GW01604969

Edition 2

Copyright Andy Brown 2017

All rights reserved. No part of this book may be reproduced, stored in a retrieval system or transmitted by any means or in any form without the prior written permission of the author, except by a reviewer who may quote brief passages in a review.

All characters appearing in this work are fictitious. Any resemblance to real persons, whether living or dead, is purely coincidental.

30130505043408

This story is dedicated to my family

# Introduction

***Transapient*** started as a short story for my daughter Emma … and then grew a bit.

Having spent thirty five years as a research engineer, I recently took early retirement, mainly to spend more time with our three children, Matthew, Emma and Katy, who are growing up so fast. Before this, as an engineer part of our work was configuring digital processing circuits to have different personalities – this concept of configurable logic has partially inspired this novel – taking it to a speculative extreme in the future (2060+) when we have found out how the human brain functions in enough detail to upload it to processing logic to create a sentient being derived from a human brain …
… a ***Transapient***.

I hope you enjoy reading and thinking about it.

# Contents

# Chapter 1

# The End

The darkness enveloped Alf Butler completely as he lay motionless; everything about him was unknown. Not only was there no light, but there was also a feeling of emptiness; a blank sheet of being awaiting an artist's first strokes of creativity. What had happened to him? Where was he? And why could he not even remember his own name? He was not physically uncomfortable, so he made his first conscious decision to stay calm and attempt to assess the unfolding situation.

A faint hum gradually became audible and Alf was soon aware of noises close by; the sound of footsteps echoing down a corridor, rhythmic beeps and the faint rustle of clothes stretching over him with barely audible shallow breathing.

"Audio input enabled," murmured a soft female voice. Who was this person? Why was it still dark? He tried to open his eyes but was unable to do so. He felt paralysed – unable to move in any way. *Stay calm* he repeated to himself. No one around him seemed to be panicking – so there was still no discernible reason why he should worry – just yet.

"Download of configuration for replicant pineal gland, insular cortex and default mode network complete," continued the voice as though following a complex recipe book. The blank sheet was being transformed into a tapestry of connections. Alf's consciousness was gradually being synthesized by billions upon billions of three dimensional connections.

"How is he doing?" a second voice asked.

“All scans show normal responses so far,” replied the now familiar female voice.

“Is the hippocampus subsystem uploaded yet?”

“Almost complete – this is going to be a bit of a shock for Alf”.

Alf. Alf? Alf! That was his name. Why had he forgotten such a basic part of his identity? A lifetime of experiences, hopes and dreams were filling a small fraction of his memory capacity and his dream like state was giving way to full awareness and consciousness, the need for answers however was also growing rapidly.

Had he been in a coma? Had he lost his memory as the result of an accident? He thought for a moment but could not recall an accident. His last recollection was an image of a face full of anguish – his wife Louisa looking into his face as she held his hand tightly and then … nothing. All recollection ceased; it felt like the events of another life time.

“Visual cortex array and visual input enabled,” said the female voice calmly. Alf became aware of a dim and fuzzy grey outline but could not make out a distinct shape.

“Let’s bring up his autonomous motor control,” suggested the second voice.

“Okay, but we must do this gradually. He will not be able to control all his anatomical peripherals to begin with,” she said with just a hint of anticipation in her voice. “Let’s start with visual and vocal subsystems”.

A surge of connections spread through Alf’s motor pathways and he felt a shudder of reflexes as bio control algorithms were initiated and began their automatic calibration routines. His eyelids twitched and slowly the dim fog lightened as the protective covers for his eyes were eased open. Gradually a shape emerged in front of him. It was the unmistakable outline of a female head and shoulders studying his every move. The female shape moved closer, slightly increasing in size and becoming animated.

"Alf? Can you hear me?" she asked staring transfixed into his dark blue eyes.

The question seemed to trigger an automatic reaction as he heard the voice again and his eyes came into focus on the source of the words. A flicker of recognition passed across his face as he looked at the person staring back at him.

"Where …?" asked Alf. He paused as he heard his own voice. It was his voice… and yet … and yet there was something unfamiliar about it which he could not quite fathom. Was that how he usually sounded? Something was odd, something felt… different.

"Hello Alf, try not to move. It's going to take some time to get you back to your old self. I'm Dr Amelia Roberts, and I will be looking after you during your stay here."

Alf's eyes surveyed her face and a stream of processed data passed to his newly established memory, recording every perceived facet of her presence; every contour of her face, the reassuring sound in her voice, the comprehension of her words, and the unfolding experience of the interaction.

"Wha-what's happened to me?" Alf demanded; the possibilities were piling up as a nagging list of uncertainty. He needed to know answers… now. Surely he was in hospital after some kind of accident. How bad was it? Was he still in one piece?

"Well, Alf." She paused as if not completely sure how to continue. "There is no easy way to tell you this. I'm afraid that yesterday on your way home you suffered a major heart attack".

“But... I cannot feel any pain, in fact I feel quite okay. Surely there has been some mistake.”

“Are you sure we should tell him straight away?” the second voice asked. Alf could not see the second person but was aware of his position as Dr Roberts looked up from his face.

“He has a right to know the truth,” she stated simply. A moment later she looked back towards Alf and continued. “No Alf. There’s no mistake. I’m sorry to say that at 8 o’clock yesterday evening you … you …,” she hesitated.

“I what?” pleaded Alf

The answer was concise, yet disturbing.

“You died.”

## Chapter 2

# The Beginning

“Sorry?” said Alf incredulously. “Is this some kind of joke? Do you mean to say that I died and was resuscitated?”

“Not in the normal sense, no”. Dr Roberts looked uncomfortably back at Alf. She was unsure how to continue and paused in thought.

“Just tell me what happened exactly,” Alf demanded.

“Okay, but it may be hard for you to take in at first.” She edged closer to Alf and he could see the strain etched on her face which had previously been hidden by her professional manner.

“We could not save your body – but we were able to take a molecular brain state matrix just prior to death.”

“You keep saying that I died!” Alf exclaimed. “But I’m here in front of you – I don’t understand what’s going on …,” His words trailed off as Dr Roberts continued.

“You may not be aware, but our capability in computing technology and understanding of brain function has progressed incredibly over the last few years. We have mapped out the 100 trillion connections between the 85 billion neurons of the human brain, and synthesised replica structures in three dimensional silicon arrays. After decades of research we have managed to map brain function onto neurological activity among neural networks.”

“Well, yes I have read some articles on Artificial Intelligence and Bio Technology,” admitted Alf. His role as a school teacher meant that he often kept up with the latest technological developments to try and keep ahead of his inquisitive students.

“Well here at the institute of Advanced Bio Computing Technology Centre or ABC-Tech as we are more commonly known, we have developed synthetic bio techniques which have fused a range of specialities, from advanced robotics, artificial intelligence, nano-technology and brain function synthesis …”

“Could you keep this simple,” pleaded Alf who did not necessarily want to hear a lecture on these state of the art developments in this field.

“Well, in simple terms, we have extracted your brain state and installed it in a synthetic three dimensional silicon array which has about ten times the number of neurons and one hundred times the connections of a normal brain. Your wife insisted that we take this pioneering step and attempt to transfer your ‘self’ onto a synthetic host body”.

“Hmm, so she couldn’t just let me rest in peace then,” Alf mused; he was trying to come to terms with this unexpected event in his life – was he still alive?

“That’s encouraging,” smiled Dr Roberts, “your humour traits look to be intact.” She made a brief note of her observations. She turned back to face him “You will have to forgive me Alf, but as you are the first transapient there is going to be a lot of interest in you.”

“The first transapient?” Alf considered his new label – the term had long been used in speculations about this possibility – the emergence of a new lifeform.

Alf took a few moments to digest this information and its implications. One day he had been an average human going about his typical human activities – and now he was the first sentient creation, a transapient. Was this just a crazy dream? Well, if it was it would be a relief to wake up to normality; but somehow he knew that as unlikely as it appeared there was no hiding from this reality. But wait he thought, he did not want to become a novel specimen for public scrutiny.

"Who knows about this?" he asked after a moment while they both sat absorbed in this first human to transapient interaction.

"We have very tight security on this development. The team involved in this project is large, but everyone involved realises the sensitivity of your existence and they have all agreed keep this quiet for the time being. It will be hard to stop this getting out in the long term, but to begin with your existence is not known outside this building – apart from your wife of course."

"Louisa." Her anguished face re-appeared in his mind. "Where is she?"

"She is just down the corridor. We just need to complete the motor control configurations and verifications before she can come in to see you."

"Okay," conceded Alf. He was keen to see a familiar face to confirm that however unlikely it seemed, this was indeed happening to him. Dr Roberts moved to a large silver dome shaped structure and initiated the remaining configurations. A faint hum changed in pitch by an octave as Alf's body was linked up to his synthetic brain.

"We have given you the shape and form of your original body," continued Dr Roberts. "We believe that this will give you anonymity for some time, as you will appear externally to be unchanged from your original body. You should be able to blend into your old life and gradually become your old self."

Self? Was he a new person who happened to share all the experiences of his old self – or was there an unbroken link to his past. He could not tell. It all felt real, and he felt the sensation of independent thought. "I think therefore I am," he muttered to himself – the proof of his own existence echoed down the centuries. Whatever he was, he was real.

Dr Roberts returned from the dome structure which had been providing all his requirements for sustainable life. But now the dome's work was complete and Dr Roberts inspected the newly configured transapient before her, free of all supporting tethers, the birth of a new independent being now complete.

"Now to begin with we have only enabled your humanoid capabilities," Dr Roberts sounded like she was telling a client about a new domestic appliance. "Once you are comfortable with that, we can then introduce some of the more advanced features which are possible with your transapient body. We just need to go through a few checks to make sure everything is functioning correctly. Please could you move your head to the left?"

Without any perceptible effort Alf turned his head to the left and took in the details of the room. A number of holographic displays were floating across the laboratory, each one was receiving attention of several people, checking these three dimensional images, periodically zooming in to particular areas to monitor detailed processes which Alf surmised were linked to his internal operation.

"That's good," reassured Dr Roberts. "Your motor function is operating normally."

"Normally?" repeated Alf. "How can you know what is normal if I am the first… transapient?"

"We have conducted many tests," Dr Roberts explained, "to check how each functional element of your design operates individually under controlled conditions, and embedded them all in an extensive range of scenarios. We are now confident that the elements can operate together in a stable manner. We have been waiting for the last few weeks for a suitable trial donor".

"You mean I am a guinea pig transapient?"

"No" smiled Dr Roberts. "We have already validated the procedure on guinea pigs. You are the first humanoid transapient".

Alf was not sure if he was honoured or unlucky. He decided to accept the facts as explained so far and continued with Dr Roberts' list of tests. He stared at each limb flex, fascinated that this was not a human body but at the same time was indistinguishable from his old body. At last he was on his feet, bending, twisting and squatting; testing out his inertial guidance. It was such a likeness to his old body that it soon felt familiar and in a few hours he was walking around the laboratory effortlessly.

"Now, there are some differences to your anatomy which you could find strange to begin with," Dr Roberts began to explain as he sat down looking at her.

"Go on," urged Alf who was keen to know any limitations which he should be aware of.

"Well, for a start, you do not have a digestive system – your energy is provided by an internal fusion reactor and your body contains a swarm of self-replicating nanobots which are like a team of maintenance staff making sure that all subsystems are operating correctly and repairing any damage that may occur in your day to day life."

"Okay I can cope with that," said Alf. "Anything else I should know about?"

“Well unlike your old body – you do not need to sleep. Your internal background computer algorithms and the nanobots take care of your mind and body so that you will never feel fatigue. Of course if you would like to shut down for a few hours as a matter of lifestyle, there is the equivalent sleep state available”

“Fine, that sounds useful,” said Alf, as he began to see that his new body did not seem to have limitations, but positive benefits.

“Oh and you don’t need to breath of course – no need for Oxygen in your body”.

“Of course,” Alf grinned. His new body had certainly dispensed with some of the obsolete features of his old body that had evolved to survive in Earth’s delicate ecosystem. “I think I’m ready to see Louisa now.” Alf’s mind had inherited all of Alf’s emotional states – at the moment it was one of anticipation at the thought of seeing his wife again.

# Chapter 3

# Reunited

"Alf ?" Louisa stared at the human form in front of her. It was her husband – but how could it be? It was like seeing a ghost. Alf had died in hospital, there had been a rush of activity and Dr Roberts had presented her with a lifeline, which she had grasped in desperation. She could not bear to be separated from Alf, her lifelong partner and soul mate. She was numbed by the shock of his death and the option being offered barely made sense – apart from the fact that it offered hope. Hope that he would return to her in some way. She would not lose him altogether.

She looked from Alf to Dr Roberts. "He … he's alive!" She rushed towards Alf, flinging her arms around him, the tears streaming down her cheeks from incredulous eyes. "But … you look exactly the same," she exclaimed. "I didn't know what to expect".

"Well I could have gone for the James Bond look, but I thought you might prefer the regular model," Alf took his wife's head in his hands and looked into her watery eyes. "It's me Louisa, I'm in here and it's great to see you." She held his hand tightly as if he might disappear if she let go – the memory of him the day before when all seemed to be at an end was still raw, and now the hope she had thought was futile had somehow been rewarded.

"Well, Mrs Butler," smiled Dr Roberts. "He's all yours now. We will be keeping an eye on him periodically by hypernet connection, just to make sure everything is working okay. We won't intrude in your domestic life, but we would like to check Alf over now and again in case any problems develop. He is a unique being, Mrs Butler. We all think he needs time to adapt to this, so we are keeping his existence quiet at the moment. As you can imagine, there will be intense media interest in him when it becomes public knowledge that the first transapient has been created".

"We will do our best, won't we Alf," Louisa beamed at Dr Roberts.

"We will," agreed Alf. "I have another chance at life and it now feels more precious than ever. I definitely don't want the world gawping at me everywhere I go," he added.

"It's been a bit of a roller coaster over the last couple of days," Louisa admitted, her face looked strained from the emotional extremes. She turned to Dr Roberts with immense gratitude, "I can never thank you enough for what you have done," she cried through sobs of relief and happiness.

Dr Roberts smiled, but felt a pang of anxiousness as her creation would soon be going into the world. She felt personally responsible for Alf's wellbeing and wondered how he would fare in a human society. The process of approval for this project had not been straight forward. Releasing an independent transapient into the world was unprecedented and there could be unknown risks. Would he be accepted by human society when his existence became widely known? Could he malfunction and become a risk to others? The design included full remote monitoring of his internal status and after much debate a shutdown command had been included to allow his internal operation to be suspended. Dr Roberts had not mentioned this fail safe feature to Alf – she was sure it was better he did not know that this level of control was available to his creators.

"Take care of him, Louisa, and please let me know if you have any problems – we are in a unique situation, so we need to be very careful with him."

"Er, transapient in the room," Alf laughed. "Don't worry; I'll look after my new body. Come on Louisa, let's go home before we have to start another round of tests".

They each embraced Dr Roberts and headed off towards the building's reception area, keen to get back to some kind of normality and if possible revert to their life together. Would it be the same? Could it be the same? Time would tell.

Louisa headed to their transportation unit and tapped in their home destination. The vehicle whirred into life and Alf and Louisa sat back as the autonomous transportation unit assessed the optimum route and accelerated down the road among a sea of other transportation units all interacting silently to fulfil a multitude of navigational requirements.

They arrived at their home a few minutes later – never had it felt better to come home than now after the two days in which life had been breathed into his new body. They closed the front door shutting out the world and sat down together – Louisa was physically exhausted; Alf looked calm and tranquil in his familiar surroundings.

"I thought I'd lost you," she whispered.

"Well, I'm not exactly the same. I hope you like the new me," he said looking at her relieved face. His mind mulled over the events of the previous days. "Come to think of it – what has happened to my old body?" he asked. "I know that they have managed to preserve my 'self' and it appears to be in tact – but my body did expire didn't it. Should there be a funeral? It would certainly raise a few eyebrows if I turned up to my own funeral," he mused.

"I hadn't thought of that," Louisa looked confused. "You haven't died totally – your mind has been preserved – but your old body shell has gone. I think we need to have a private ceremony to celebrate your human life – but then you would be officially dead and it might cause problems in adopting your own identity if there was a record of your death. Oh my goodness!"

"You're right," said Alf who was unsure what to suggest. Maybe we should have a word with Dr Roberts. She might have a suggestion. Alf activated the holophone and a few seconds later a hologram of Dr Roberts appeared in the room.

"Oh, hello Alf and Louisa," Dr Roberts looked surprised and concerned. "Any problems?"

"Well not with the new me" said Alf. "We were just wondering what is going to happen to the old me – my old body that is."

Dr Roberts looked surprised at this query. "Well, we have it in storage at the moment and thought it best to wait until your existence becomes official – whenever that may be. And then we can have your humanoid funeral without highlighting your new transapient state".

"Oh okay" said Alf. "Looks like you have considered this already. It has raised some complicated issues having two bodies to think about."

"Yes" agreed Dr Roberts. "For now I suggest that you try to forget that you are a transapient, and concentrate on keeping your true identity quiet. If that is all, I'll say good night to you both."

The holograms of Alf and Louisa that were in the laboratory faded from view and Dr Roberts returned to her work in the adjacent room. There on a bed lay a familiar looking figure – someone who Dr Roberts had already got to know quite well. The figure on the bed stared up at Dr Roberts.

"Where …?" began the figure pausing at the sound of his own voice.

“Hello Alf, try not to move. It’s going to take some time to get you back to your old self. I’m Dr Amelia Roberts, and I will be looking after you during your stay here.”

## Chapter 4

# Another New Beginning

"What on earth have you done?" demanded Dr James. His face was full of disbelief as he glared at Dr Roberts. "That transapient body was reserved as a potential replacement, not to be configured as an additional being. The terms of our license agreement clearly state that we are only allowed to release one transapient into the world."

"Exactly," countered Dr Roberts. "Which is why I do not intend releasing this transapient from our laboratory. This is far too important a development not to be able to study a transapient at close quarters under strictly controlled conditions. We need a working model here where we will be able to check out so many environmental scenarios and observe his behaviour in the laboratory instead of reacting to the random events that might occur outside."

"But he is a sentient being for heaven's sake – not some inanimate clockwork object you can pick up and put down on a whim. How do you think he will feel being effectively imprisoned in here? Don't transapients inherit human rights? And what about his wife? He will want to see her! How will that work? Can't you see how complicated this situation is now becoming. He is more than just an identical twin – he shares all memories up until the point when the molecular brain state matrix was captured. He is effectively the 'same' being."

"As I said, his environment will be under our control – his wife will not exist in the new environment."

"So you are going to lie to him? I must say, that is not a good start for human - transapient relations. Surely his rights to liberty should be respected. Do you think he will trust you when he finds out the truth?" Dr James implored.

"We need to know his operating limits" countered Dr Roberts. "You know we have never tested all his functional elements operating together. We may discover an instability that has not been fully simulated and analysed. I am thinking of the long term wellbeing of both transapients and human society. I'm sorry that he must sacrifice his liberty to this end but I believe it will have a net benefit. And as you know, transapients do not currently have any legal status."

"Well if they do not then maybe they should have. I think you are treading a very slippery path Dr Roberts, and I do not wish to be part of it." Dr James stormed out of the room leaving Dr Roberts to contemplate the second transapient's future. She knew that there were many moral issues to this creation but still felt that on balance she was taking the correct course of action.

She returned to attend to Alf#2. With Dr James concerns still ringing in her ears she decided that he was partially right – the new transapient had a right to know the truth however painful or complicated that might appear to him. With the possibility of distressing revelations, it would be important that Alf#2 trusted her, and that could only really be by sharing the truth with him.

Alf#2 looked up at her. "A transapient?" he asked. "But I didn't know that was even possible. I've read about various developments, but I had not appreciated just how feasible it had become. Does this mean I am the first of a new lifeform?" enquired Alf#2.

Dr Roberts shifted uncomfortably in her seat and avoided his gaze. Alf#2 knew the answer before she spoke.

"Not exactly" she said and was struggling to find a way to present Alf#2 with a palatable truth.

"What do you mean, 'not exactly'?" he asked. "Either I am the first transapient or I am not. Are there others like me?"

"Yes," conceded Dr Roberts. "There is one other transapient in existence".

"Just one?" Alf#2 digested this fact and appeared to accept it. "So there are just two of us; a bit like Adam and Eve," he mused.

"Well more like Adam and Adam," Dr Roberts could not deny him the facts, but how would he take it.

"So there is another male transapient like me." Alf#2 noted. At least he was not a lone member of this emergent lifeform. But he could see that Dr Roberts still had something else to add. "And..?"

"The first transapient is not just like you," she hesitated, "He is identical to you in nearly every conceivable way." The bare truth was laid out and now she would need to deal with all its consequences.

Alf#2 was finding it hard to take in this latest piece of information. He now knew he had a perfectly identical twin. It was like finding he had a long lost sibling.

Dr Roberts elaborated. "Just to be clear, the first transapient is effectively you with all your experiences up to the time your molecular brain state matrix was captured. This captured 'self' has been installed in two transapients, so you are more alike than any human twins."

"So you can store a personality and install it in more than one body?" said Alf#2 checking his understanding.

"Exactly," confirmed Dr Roberts. "And your new body also contains a 'black box' recorder that will enable your 'self' to be extracted and installed into a new transapient if this necessary at any time in the future.” Dr Roberts looked proud as she explained the transapients endurance capabilities.

“And … what has happened to the first transapient?” asked Alf#2 with more than hint of ‘self’ interest.

Again Dr Roberts looked uncomfortable. It was difficult to tell Alf#2 the truth, but it had to be done. “He - he’s at home with your wife…” the words trailed off as soon as she had started the reply; she knew that this sounded just bizarre.

## Chapter 5

# A Life Sentence

"Okay," said Alf#2. "So now I know about what has happened to me or should I say us." He was still trying to come to terms with the fact he had not only been transformed, but totally replicated. "I now have some questions to ask you Dr Roberts."

"Sure, I understand" she readied herself for a barrage of possible questions.

"Do you understand?" Alf#2 looked thoughtful. "My biggest question is quite simple… why? Why make two of us from one human life?"

Dr Roberts had already been challenged about this by Dr James, but this time the challenger could not escape from the situation. He was the subject of concern and Dr Roberts was not sure how this transapient would respond. "We are at the dawn of a new era" began Dr Roberts. "The ability to create a sentient being equivalent to a human, and in many ways superior to a human, is a momentous event. The first transapient is now starting his life, albeit a continuation of his human life, outside the controlled environment of this laboratory. Our operating license only allows one transapient to be released – but we needed another transapient we could evaluate here. We could not know how a transapient would cope with every situation that arises so we had to create a replica to allow any anomalous behaviour to be analysed and then rectified."

Alf#2 considered his situation for a few seconds. "So I am to be kept here like a caged animal that you can prod and study – in fact I will effectively be imprisoned while my other self enjoys a new life with… with … Louisa." He could barely bring himself to say her name. It was as though she had been taken from him – and he would just become a test case to reinforce his *brother*'s wellbeing.

"You have a crucial role in this development," said Dr Roberts. "I was hoping that you would help us introduce transapients into the world with your unique capabilities".

"But I'm not unique am I," exclaimed Alf#2. "I'm not sure I am willing to go along with this. Or has my free will been dropped in the transformation. I'm sorry Dr Roberts but I need to see my wife – she means everything to me."

Dr Roberts felt mixed emotions – she was disappointed that Alf#2 did not want to cooperate, but at the same time she admired his independent outlook – he was truly attempting to steer his own destiny. She looked into the same blue eyes as the original transapient. "Alf, we are bound by the terms of our licence agreement. We are not allowed to release you into the world. I'm afraid that you must stay here."

"Then let's get the agreement changed," retorted Alf#2. "Holding a sentient being against their will must be wrong. Don't transapients have rights just the same as humans? We are after all directly descended or transformed from humans. Do we not inherit those rights?"

Dr Roberts found herself sympathetic to Alf#2's point of view, just as Dr James had swayed her to follow an honest relationship with this new being. "The law is sadly lagging behind events at the moment" admitted Dr Roberts. "Transapients do not currently have any legal status – mainly because up to now there has been no existing transapients."

"Then speaking as a representative of transapients – even though there are only two of us – I think the time is right for this to be addressed, and in my particular case, as soon as possible. I am effectively the same person as the Alf last week. You would not be able to detain him against his will – so if I am still Alf, you should not be able to detain me either".

Dr Roberts was now completely won over by Alf#2's determination. Morally, if not legally she agreed with him. "I can see your point," conceded Dr Roberts. "Look, I am going to have to discuss this with our legal department to see what can be done. Please bear with me while I explore the possibilities."

Alf#2 could see that Dr Roberts was being sincere. She had gained his trust and he began to feel hopeful of a resolution. Otherwise he would be condemned to a life sentence within this building – his spirit would not contemplate this outcome.

Dr Roberts made her way through the labyrinth of corridors to Dr James' office. She knocked gently on the door and entered. Dr James looked up from the hologram he was studying and frowned. "Hello Dr Roberts," he said stiffly "I was not expecting to see you again after this morning."

"I am really sorry about that – you were right all along and I can see that now," apologised Dr Roberts.

"Really," said Dr James raising one eyebrow in surprise. "Well I'm glad you have seen sense. Have you de-activated him yet," he looked relieved that Dr Roberts had come around to his reasoning.

"No I haven't, and I don't intend to. Look Dr James, I followed your advice about being honest with Alf#2, but now he is refusing to accept confinement within the laboratory."

"That's hardly surprising," said Dr James. "You should have anticipated that response. Why not just deactivate him and we will be back to where we were yesterday – one transapient and one spare synthetic body," suggested Dr James.

"Now listen Dr James" said Dr Roberts indignantly "you put me onto the correct moral path, so I don't think we should now commit a moral crime by terminating a sentient life".

"Well I did tell you it was a mistake installing a second transapient. You've let the genie out of the bottle what are you going to do now?" Dr James asked.

Dr Roberts sat down and looked skywards as if seeking inspiration. "He wants us to create a law giving transapients equal rights to humans, he wants to be able to leave the building, and he wants to see his wife, Louisa."

"Quite a demanding transapient isn't he," remarked Dr James. "This is certainly opening up a can of worms".

"Well, now that transapients do exist, isn't it time that these issues were addressed? The technological advances have outstripped the legal framework needed to guide the consequences of sentient being creation." Dr Roberts paused. "You know, Alf#2 pointed out that he should inherit the human rights of his old self, and I am inclined to agree with him. Do you think we could run it past our legal department? This is beyond my area of expertise."

"Okay," said Dr James. "I will set up a meeting this evening. But it will not be a quick process once the legal department get involved. Could we not suspend Alf#2 using the shutdown command while this is being sorted out?"

"We could do, but this would yet again be imposing our will on him – and we will probably need him as a key witness in legal proceedings. No, the shutdown command was for emergencies – although this is serious, it has not got to that level yet."

“I can see that your moral compass is back on track now,” commented Dr James. “Perhaps we could concede to one of his demands though – how about letting him see his wife here?”

Dr Roberts could see this was a possibility, but Louisa was unaware of Alf#2’s existence, as was Alf#1 for that matter. How on earth was she going to explain Alf#2, and how would Louisa react to having two husbands – and how would the two Alfs regard each other?

# Chapter 6

# The Visit

Louisa was beginning to relax after the unbelievable events of the previous days. She had her husband back and though she knew he was not exactly the same – it felt the same. She still could not get used to him not eating or breathing though. These features of human existence were so basic that it was difficult to accept that he did not need food or air.

Alf#1 had gone out for a walk by himself. He wanted to check out his in built navigation system and more importantly he wanted to blend in to everyday life – would anyone stop and stare at him or would he just pass on by without a second look? Alf#1 was hoping for the latter. The more he could practice just being himself, the more confident he would feel in new situations. He felt it was imperative to keep his status as the first and only transapient quiet for as long as possible while he adapted to his extended life.

Meanwhile Louisa was winding down after doing her daily exercise routine. A cool glass of water in her hand she sat down and felt herself begin to doze as her body tensions eased and her muscles relaxed after their recent exertion.

The familiar sound of the holophone brought her rapidly out of her tranquil state. She rolled off the sofa and accepted the call. A hologram of Dr Roberts appeared in front of her with an apologetic look on her face. "Hello Louisa, how are you?" said Dr Roberts.

"Fine thanks," replied Louisa. "So far so good. Alf's just gone out exploring, testing out his navigation – he's like a kid with a new toy." Louisa smiled.

“That’s good,” said Dr Roberts. “Louisa, we need to see you at the laboratory as soon as you can make it”.

“Oh, okay. Can’t we deal with it over the hypernet?” asked Louisa who was just getting used to normal domestic life again. The laboratory had been a life saver, but it was still associated in her mind with emotional turmoil.

“Sorry, no we can’t. We need to see you personally about Alf and there are certain things which we need to keep confidential. Can you come by yourself?”

“Yes, Alf is going shopping later to keep himself immersed in public environments, so I’ll pop over then.” Louisa felt a bit uneasy about this request – what did they want to talk about that they could not discuss over hypernet or in Alf’s presence. “See you soon,” Dr Roberts’ hologram faded from view and Louisa was left wondering what this mysterious meeting was all about.

Several hours later Louisa was back at the laboratory in front of Dr Roberts. “Thank you for coming so promptly,” said Dr Roberts.

“That’s okay,” said Louisa, “but I am intrigued about what it is you need to see me for.”

“Well Mrs Butler, there have been some developments here which are quite significant.”

“Is anything wrong with Alf?” Louisa asked with concern.

“No, he is fine,” reassured Dr Roberts, “but something has happened here which could affect both you and Alf.”

“Go on,” urged Louisa feeling slightly less distressed, but still wanting to know what Dr Roberts was about to reveal.

"Well, we have configured a second transapient that was intended as a reference model for conducting more detailed evaluations."

"Oh, I see," said Louisa who was now wondering why this fact should directly affect herself or Alf. She could see that once the process for creating a transapient had been validated, she had living proof of that; then it would be natural to repeat the process for checking reliable reproduction.

Dr Roberts hesitated. "Mrs Butler, the transapient is a reproduction based on Alf."

It took a few moments for this last critical piece of information to register in Louisa's mind. And then gradually the implications of this development in the context of her current situation; living with a transapient which was one of two editions, began to sink in.

"But why use Alf's personality?" she asked trying not to envisage all the possible consequences of having two husbands.

"Well we wanted an exact replica so that we could test this transapient under conditions which your Alf might encounter, before they arise. We needed to be sure that there were no problems in advance."

"But Alf would never want to become a lab specimen!" Louisa cried.

"I know," Dr Roberts conceded. "He is adamant that he wants his freedom and we are currently exploring that with our legal department. But he has also asked to see you."

Louisa looked bewildered. How could she split herself between two identical beings. She felt very sorry for Alf#2 who had the prospect of being confined even though he was quite innocent. "I will see him now," she said with a new resolve considering the injustice of his situation. Dr Roberts lead the way to an adjacent room where Alf#2 sat quietly. He looked up when Louisa entered the room and a flood of memories came pouring into his mind, with the last being her anguished face as she gripped his hand.

“Louisa!” Alf#2 cried. It was like a replay of their earlier reunion with Alf#1. But Louisa could not help thinking about Alf#1, the one who she was now sharing her life, the one who was currently going about quite ordinary activities in his extraordinary body. Alf#2 looked into her eyes. “It’s me Louisa, I’m in here and it’s great to see you.”

## Chapter 7

# Two's Company

Louisa looked backed at Alf#2, tears flowing once more. "This is just too confusing," she declared as Dr Roberts joined them. "Surely you can't keep him here – it's like a prison to him." Alf#2 waited for Dr Roberts' reply.

"We are exploring possibilities at the moment – but we cannot release him until we have sorted out the legal aspects," said Dr Roberts.

"If there is anything we can do to help," said Louisa, "please let us know. I'm afraid I must go home as Alf will be back from his shopping trip soon".

"How am I doing in the outside world," asked Alf#2.

"You're fine," answered Louisa "Just fine." She looked away knowing that Alf#2 must be envious of his other self who was living his life and, as if to add to his sense of loss, sharing it with his wife.

"Please come back soon," pleaded Alf#2. "I need to see you".

Louisa was torn. How could she deny her husband this request? The two Alfs were merging in her mind – they both needed her but how could she manage two identical husbands?

"I'll be back," said Louisa finally.

"You've been watching those old Terminator movies again haven't you" said Alf#2. His sense of humour traits were also intact - but he felt a twinge of sadness as she turned to go … to go back to his other self.

As she reached the main entrance Louisa turned to Dr Roberts. “How long do you think it will take to sort out his legal status?”

Dr Roberts did not want raise any false hopes “I cannot say for sure,” she replied “This is an unprecedented situation. We may need a trial case to address the legal rights of all transapients now they exist and that could be a lengthy process. I think our best hope is to request a change to our license agreement so that we can release two transapients, instead of just one. Either way it will not be very soon.”

“Okay, thank you Dr Roberts, I’ll discuss this with Alf#1 when I get home.”

“Are you sure that’s a good idea?” asked Dr Roberts.

“Absolutely,” replied Louisa. “I know Alf, and he would not want things kept from him.”

Dr Roberts shook her head. The can of worms was spreading relentlessly.

*

Louisa arrived home her head still spinning with the latest revelations. When Alf#1 arrived she saw him in a new light; not as a unique person, but as one of a pair, identical in nearly every conceivable way. Only the experiences of the last two days separated them. Alf#1 was just one day ‘older’ than Alf#2.

“Are you okay?” asked Alf#1. He could see the distress on her face as he walked in the room.

“Well, not exactly,” replied Louisa her mind flitting between the Alf before her and the recent memory of Alf#2. “I had a meeting at the laboratory this afternoon," she began, "and something has happened which will affect us both".

Alf#1 awaited the details – this sounded serious. Was there a problem with his transformation? "Whatever it is, I'm sure we can sort it out together," he said trying to reassure her.

She took a deep breath and then continued. "Dr Roberts has created another transapient using your molecular brain state matrix …," she could not continue, but she did not need to. Alf#1 had immediately digested this new information and he shuddered as the implication of this fact hit him. He was no longer unique – his 'self' had been split into two and he could see that Louisa had already been affected by Alf#2's existence.

"Did you … see him," Alf#1 asked. He already knew the answer, but needed to know more.

"Yes," said Louisa. She felt a twinge of guilt that she had seen Alf#2 without Alf#1. "He does not want to stay at the laboratory, but until Dr Roberts has clarified his legal status he can't be released."

Alf#1 had a fair idea how Alf#2 would be feeling. From his own experience in the laboratory, he had been very relieved to escape from the endless tests – and that had only been one day. The prospect of indefinite detention would be extremely unsettling. After a few moments in which Louisa was uncertain of how Alf#1 would react, he looked up into her worried face. "We must help him," said Alf#1 finally.

Louisa took Alf#1's hand and squeezed it gently. "Thank you," she said grateful that Alf#1 was actively defending Alf#2. "But how can we help him?" asked Louisa.

Alf#1 had already assessed various options. "I have a plan, but you must trust me to follow it through. It will work better if you don't know the details for now. Please could you arrange a visit with Dr Roberts for us to go and see Alf#2?"

Louisa looked quizzically at Alf#1. "Okay," she said slowly trying to imagine what Alf#1 had in mind. "For both of us?"

"Yes, we need to see Alf#2 as soon as possible."

Louisa activated the holophone and a few seconds later the projection of Dr Roberts appeared before them. "Hello Louisa, hello Alf," Dr Roberts greeted them. "How are you both?"

"We are fine," said Louisa. "Dr Roberts, can we arrange to visit Alf#2. We would like to give him our support while he is waiting for the legal process to be sorted out."

Dr Roberts looked pleased. "That should be fine. How about tomorrow morning?" she asked.

"We'll be there," said Louisa calmly. "See you tomorrow."

The hologram faded away and Louisa turned to Alf#1. "I hope you know what you are doing," she said. But she knew she could trust him – he had always been there for her, and even in his new body she felt that whatever plan it was, he would have considered her wellbeing beyond anything else.

Alf#1 went through the idea in his mind like a chess player analysing a multitude of possible outcomes, seeking out a strategy which would maximize the chances of success. Yes, this should work he told himself.

# Chapter 8

# Double Cross

Alf#1 and Louisa arrived at the laboratory the next day as planned. Dr Roberts greeted them at the reception area and they made their way to the familiar laboratory where Alf#1's new life had begun on April 23$^{rd}$ 2059 and Alf#2's new life had begun on April 24$^{th}$ 2059. Dr Roberts could not suppress her intrigue at this meeting "This is another first for us" she said enthusiastically, her face brimming with pride "The first transapient to transapient meeting."

They were gathered in a meeting room just off the main laboratory, the walls were covered in various awards that had been bestowed on ABC-Tech, the organisation that had brought together the advanced technologies which had culminated in the creation of the first two transapients. This latest development was still not publicly known, although some technical commentators had long speculated that this could well be possible in the future – but for now they did not know it had just been achieved.

Louisa on the other hand felt quite apprehensive about the meeting. The two Alfs were practically the same person. She was confused. Was she married to both of them or neither of them? Had that marriage died with the human Alf? Till death us do part… but this had not been a normal death – everything that made Alf Alf had been preserved and regenerated… twice. She was so grateful to have had the chance to keep Alf's life in this sentient being but the arrival of another Alf had highlighted a difference between her human and transapient husbands. He could be replicated as though his hologram had suddenly become solid. Where was the uniqueness of 'self'?

While she struggled with these concepts, she became aware that Alf#2 had entered the room. The two Alfs stood in front of each other studying their respective faces as though staring into a mirror. But the image before each of them was not virtual – each was a solid transapient, a product of technological achievements which had given humans the ability to create superior beings.

"Hello Alf," said Alf#1 breaking the ice with a greeting that sounded quite peculiar to his own audio input.

"Good to see you both," said Alf#2 "I'm pleased you could come." Dr Roberts stood to one side transfixed by the sight of her two creations talking amiably. Alf#2 looked at Alf#1's eyes as he spoke and noticed an almost imperceptible movement in his eyelid. He was now quite familiar with his and hence Alf#1's body and this movement, which was not noticeable to the human eye was not a normal feature under these conditions. In a split second Alf#2 had analysed the eyelid movement which had 32 states he soon realised that these were being used as a text messaging channel.

Alf#2 soon made sense of these small movements – Alf#1 was sending him a covert message in real time even while he was speaking to him.

*** *hello alf i need to talk to you privately about your situation* *** Alf#2 immediately understood what Alf#1 was doing and while they conversed with each other audibly, exchanging amazement at how alike they were and sympathising with Alf#2's predicament, they carried on a separate visual conversation with Alf#2 using the same eyelid movements to maintain the private dialogue.

*** *okay go ahead* *** Alf#2 responded with the tiniest flicker of his eyelid.

*** subtract one from your serial number *** Alf#1's message to Alf#2 was clear – this was a serial number embedded in Alf#2's body – the only way he could easily be identified and distinguished from Alf#1 with local sensors. Simultaneously Alf#1 had incremented his serial number by one. In the bat of an eye they had swapped serial numbers and hence identities.

Meanwhile Alf#2 who was now talking and texting at the same time, also knew what Alf#1's plan was. They were about to swap places. But how could they do that with both Dr Roberts and Louisa watching their every move – or at least the audible ones. They needed a diversion.

*** *we need a diversion* *** Alf#1 texted with a flicker of his eyelids.

*** *i know* *** concurred Af#2.

Alf#1 texted his plan to Alf#2 and Alf#2 acknowledged the plan with the briefest of flickers back to Alf#1 – they were ready to execute it.

"… and so I have to wait until the legal department have explored all the possible avenues. I I'll just have to …," Alf#2 froze in mid-sentence. Not only did his voice stop abruptly but his whole body became rigid and inanimate, without a hint of movement.

Dr Roberts stared at Alf#2 with concern. "Alf, Alf what's wrong?" They all gathered round willing him to move but it was as if he were a wax model of a human, still and lifeless.

"Don't move anything – I need to get Dr James to help me diagnose Alf#2's problem." Dr Roberts ran from the room and Louisa watched her anxiously, her attention momentarily distracted from her two transapients. In that fleeting moment the two Alfs took their window of opportunity and swapped places, Alf#1 stood in Alf#2's place with the same frozen expression, while Alf#2 took on the posture of Alf#1 – it was a perfect swap. Louisa was aware of some movement from her peripheral vision, but she assumed that the movement was just Alf#1 – she had no inkling that they had both moved.

A few moments later Dr Roberts and Dr James came running back into the room to attend to Alf#2. The three figures in the room were in exactly the same position as Dr Roberts had left them. The escape plan was working. Louisa's ignorance of the plan helped as she and the animate Alf#2 were ushered out of the room by Dr Roberts, leaving Alf#1 to the attentions of Dr James. "We need to check Alf#2 over to see what is going on," said Dr Roberts briskly. "I'm afraid that we will have to end the visit today".

*Perfect* thought both Alfs simultaneously.

## Chapter 9

# Confessions

“I hope they can find out Alf#2’s problem,” said Louisa when they were back at home. Alf#2 had been uncharacteristically quiet on the journey back and Louisa assumed that he was thinking about the incident in the laboratory too.

“There is nothing wrong with him,” said Alf#2 quietly.

“How can you be sure of that?” asked Louisa in surprise.

“Because it was part of the plan,” confessed Alf#2.

The plan. Louisa new Alf#1 had a plan in mind but as far as she could see nothing extraordinary had happened at the meeting – apart from …

“Alf#2 freezing was part of the plan?” said Louisa “But how did Alf#2 even know there was a plan to start with?”

“We set up a covert text channel to send instructions while we talked,” explained Alf#2. “The diversion caused by freezing gave us enough time to swap positions and …”

“And you are Alf#2!” exclaimed Louisa. “I would never have known. So Alf#1 has sacrificed his liberty for you.” She blinked in amazement at Alf#2, still trying to come to terms that this was another incarnation of her husband. “So what happens now?” she asked assuming that there might be a follow-on strategy having executed their undercover swap.

“Well, to tell you the truth, we did not have time to discuss what we should do next. Alf#1 caught me by surprise and it was all I could do to go along with the events that unfolded.”

Louisa began to consider their situation. “If they find out that you are here instead of Alf#1 they will probably try to take you back to the laboratory. On the other hand, if they don’t find out, then Alf#1 will be stuck in the same position as you.”

“Exactly,” said Alf#2. “We must think of a way to help Alf#1 – but we cannot keep swapping identities like this. We need a long term solution….”.

*

Just as suddenly as Alf had frozen all activity in his transapient body, he resumed his demeanour as though nothing had happened “ … be patient I suppose,” Alf#1 concluded Alf#2’s half of the conversation that had occurred several hours previously and then looked around as if trying to locate Louisa and Alf#1. Dr Roberts and Dr James, who had been initiating diagnostic sensor analysis of Alf’s brain activity jumped back in surprise.

“Alf!” cried Dr Roberts. “How are you feeling? You just blanked out for several hours”.

“Did I?” Alf#1 replied as if in astonishment. “How did that happen?”

“We were hoping you might provide us with some clues yourself” said Dr James, recovering his composure after the shock of Alf’s sudden awakening.

“I’m sorry, Dr James,” said Alf#1, “but I was in the middle of a conversation with Louisa when suddenly they just … disappeared.”

“It looks like something caused the suspension of all your activities for the last three hours,” said Dr Roberts, trying to find some trace of anomaly in her instrument readings. "As far as I can tell at the moment, all your functions are operating normally. There is no obvious sign of any malfunction," she frowned, puzzling over the problem. In her profession she was used to bugs occurring in sophisticated equipment and it could often take some detailed detective work to get to the source of the problem, but in this case there were no residual symptoms which she could use as a starting point for analysis.

"We will need to keep you under observation," said Dr James. "An unknown anomaly like this is serious for both you and Louisa's Alf." He turned to Dr Roberts, "I think we have no alternative but to recall Louisa's Alf until we get to the bottom of this," he concluded.

"I agree," said Dr Roberts. "If the transapient design has an emergent fault like this then we cannot let him continue to be out in the public domain."

Alf#1 was now concerned that the plan was crumbling. Instead of liberating Alf#2, they could end up both being kept at the laboratory. "But Louisa's Alf has not shown any signs of this problem" said Alf#1, desperate to avoid the detention of his other self.

"We cannot take any risks, Alf. You are the most advanced machine ever created and you are identical to Louisa's, Alf. We must keep you both here until we know what caused your blackout."

Alf#1 could see that she was adamant. He needed a Plan B, and quickly.

"Dr Roberts?" Alf#1 said quietly.

"Yes Alf, what is it?" Dr Roberts stopped her intense discussions with Dr James and came over to Alf#1.

"I have a confession to make," he said slowly.

“Go on,” urged Dr Roberts.

“Well, I have been conducting a study of human behaviour and one of my psychometric tests was to see how human’s respond to unsolvable problems – so I initiated an event which tests this using myself as part of the test.”

Dr Roberts was lost for words. Had this transapient turned the tables on its creators? Was it now considering humans as a curiosity with their limited capacity and analysing them as a human might examine a primitive organism under a microscope?

“So you imitated a blackout to test our reaction?” Dr Roberts was digesting this revelation. It fitted with the observations – no anomalous conditions had been detected. For her it was a fascinating development.

“So why have you confessed to this ‘test’ now?” asked Dr James, who realised they had been anxiously looking for solutions to a problem that did not exist.”

“I felt that the consequences of this test might be more far reaching than expected, so I thought it best to make you aware of my status and terminate the test prematurely.”

“Well I’m relieved that you did,” said Dr Roberts. “It seems that our creation has a well-developed sense of independent thought.”

## Chapter 10

# Liberty Licence

Alf#2 and Louisa were still pondering the possible ways of getting Alf#1 released from the laboratory. “There must be some way we can help him” said Louisa who realised that she had been in exactly this predicament with Alf#2 a couple of days before. She shook her head in frustration and Alf#2 shrugged his shoulders in sympathy.

The deliberations were interrupted by a call on the holophone and Dr Roberts’ hologram appeared in front of them. “Good evening, Louisa and Alf” said Dr Roberts “I have an important update on Alf#2’s condition.” Alf#2 immediately concluded that Dr Roberts had not discovered Alf’s true identity.

“How is he?” Louisa asked – she had been wondering how Alf#1 would prolong their secret body swap.

“Actually he seems to be totally fine – you’re not going to believe this but the freezing was an elaborate hoax designed to test our reactions.”

“No!” said Louisa convincingly. “That’s unbelievable,” she felt a twinge of guilt in her declaration as she knew it was not true. “Well he certainly had us worried,” at least this statement was true she thought.

“I think Alf#2 realises that now. He would like you to come in so he can apologise to you in person. Is tomorrow okay for you both?”

Louisa and Alf#2 nodded in agreement “That’s fine,” said Louisa. “We’ll be there.”

*

The next day Louisa and Alf#2 arrived at the laboratory and were soon joined by Alf#1. Louisa watched the two Alfs who maintained eye contact throughout the conversation, and she knew that there were unheard exchanges taking place between them. Dr Roberts was relieved that this visit appeared to be completed without any unexpected events.

Various snippets of news were discussed, the most significant of which was that the legal department had arranged a hearing to apply for an extension to the current license which only allowed the release of one transapient outside the laboratory.

"... and Alf#2 has insisted that he represent the case for extension himself," said Dr Roberts as they concluded their visit.

*

When Alf#2 and Louisa returned home she could not wait to hear what the two Alfs had been discussing privately in their latest meeting.

"Alf#1 asked us not to try anything else to release him," said Alf#2. "He is confident he will be able to convince the licensing committee that an extension is appropriate."

"So he has a Plan B for legitimate release?" asked Louisa. "It would be better to be legally released rather than an elaborate escape with all sorts of consequences for everyone. When is the hearing?"

"Next week" said Alf#2. "And he said we need to go along to provide supporting evidence."

"Really? I hope Plan B goes as well as the swap plan," Louisa mused.

*

The day of the hearing arrived and Alf#1 stood at the focus of a semi-circular arrangement of desks together with Dr Roberts. Nine committee members sat around the table all gazing at Alf#1 who showed no signs of wilting under this scrutiny. A tall man with piercing blue eyes sat at the centre of the committee – he was clearly the chair person and after several seconds elapsed as a prelude to the hearing, the tall man addressed the room in a deep clear voice.

“Ladies and Gentlemen, we …”

Alf#1 had raised his hand. “Objection Mr Chairman”.

The tall man raised one eyebrow as he had hardly begun his opening statement. “Yes Mr Butler – I’m not usually interrupted this early in the proceedings.”

“I would respectfully ask that you include transapients in your collective address” said Alf#1, “and that I am specifically addressed as Mr Butler#2”.

Louisa looked down biting her lip wondering how this confrontational approach would be received by the committee. It certainly had the effect of raising the interest level among all members who now sat motionless while waiting for the case to be presented.

“Apologies Mr Butler#2, you are quite right,” the chairman conceded. “You represent a new sentient lifeform and I should have included your title among the list of participants. Allow me to start again.” He coughed and started the proceedings again, “Ladies, Gentlemen and Transapients,” he paused in case there were any further objections to this revised address. “We are gathered here to review an application to extend the licence for the number of transapients allowed outside ABC-Tech Laboratory from one to two." There was a murmur of concern among the committee members. "As you all know, this transapient is the second of two so far created. The first transapient called Alf Butler already resides with his human wife and is gradually integrating with humans. The license was limited to one transapient because this is an unprecedented situation – we need to be very confident that the introduction of transapients into human society is carefully and sensitively managed." The chairman paused again to allow the current situation to sink in before continuing. "Mr Alf Butler#2, you have requested to present your own case for this license amendment, please proceed."

Alf#1 walked slowly around in front of the committee members and then back to the focal point of the semi-circle turning to face them. "Good morning," he began. "As you all know, I am a Transapient, a new lifeform derived from a human being. In fact I can remember all my human life experiences just as any of you can remember yours. I am a sentient being, able to feel and respond to sensations even beyond the range of human senses. I am also able to make deductions, propose solutions to problems and present cases for hearings."

The committee attention was held; listening to Alf#1 they were fascinated by his human qualities, witnessing first hand his ability to make reasoned arguments.

"You are clearly an impressive individual," noted the chairman, "but the technology is still in its infancy – you are the first of your kind and we must consider the risks of introducing transapients into human society."

"I appreciate your concerns," said Alf#1. "Introducing transapients into human society *is* a significant step in the history of evolution. I have inherited human characteristics, but I have been produced by man-made materials instead of a biological recipe defined by the genome. Humans and their descendants, transapients, are now in control of their future. They can adapt themselves to nearly any environment, instead of relying on natural selection which originally led to the emergence of human beings."

Alf#1 continued with his case, returning to the concerns raised by the chairman. "You are wise to limit the introduction of transapients into society and I agree that the limit should be one individual." The committee began to wonder if Alf#1 was changing his mind. "My main argument for this case, however, is that the first two transapients were derived from the *same* individual. They are practically the same person in every respect, with shared human memories and identical construction. I can understand the concerns regarding transapients derived from *different* individuals where the variability of the transfer could be uncertain, but in our case – we are so alike, even more so than identical human twins".

The chairman addressed Dr Roberts who had been watching with pride as her creation presented his reasoned arguments. "Dr Roberts, is their scope for variability between twin transapients?"

"Their construction is identical," Dr Roberts replied. "They have exactly the same body and synthetic brain matrix. They are initiated from exactly the same molecular brain state matrix. So at creation they are duplicate beings. After that their experiences will be different, but they will respond in the same way to the same sensory inputs taking into account accumulated experiences. In this sense the risk of introducing two identical transapients is no different to one, apart from the different experiences of each. The experience rate will be double that of a single transapient, but otherwise there is no difference between a single transapient being in society for twice as long as two twin transapients."

Alf#1 nodded to Dr Roberts in acknowledgement of her support as the committee discussed the case among themselves. He then raised his hand in order to gain attention of the chairman again. “Yes, Mr Butler#2, you have more to add?”

“I have Mr Chairman, I would like to call upon my twin transapient and our human wife to conclude our case.”

“Very well,” said the chairman “Please proceed.”

Alf#2 and Louisa stepped up adjacent to Alf#1. “Thank you for joining us” said Alf#1. He looked directly at Alf#2 and sent a visual message with the briefest of flickers

*** *the truth* *** Alf#1 texted

Alf#2 had no time to respond “Please could you tell the committee your name” Alf#1 addressed Alf#2.

“Certainly.” said Alf#2 “My name is Alf Butler ….#2”.

Dr Roberts gasped, “But that is not true, you are Alf#2” she said to Alf#1.

“I assure you,” said Alf#1 “he is Alf#2 and I am Alf#1”.

The committee started to talk to each other in hushed voices.

“As I have said, we are effectively the same person,” said Alf#1, “and during our first meeting we agreed to swap places as Alf#2 was not happy with his confinement – as equally am I not happy with my confinement now.”

Dr Roberts suddenly realised what had happened in the meeting between the two Alfs – the unexplained freezing black out – the clever role reversal between the transapients, it all made sense now.

Alf#1 continued. “For the last week Alf#2 has been living with Louisa and I have been at the laboratory. I contend that we have both had probationary periods outside the laboratory and at different times Dr Roberts and Louisa have been unaware of any difference between us."

Further discussion ensued among the committee - the latest revelation had caused quite a stir among them.

Alf#1 raised his hand again. The chairman nodded his acknowledgement and the committee fell silent.

"I would like to propose a small revision to the amended licence – ABC Tech should be allowed to release just one model transapient, that is to say transapients derived from the same source molecular brain matrix".

There was a murmur of approval from the committee and the chairman checked the combined feedback from all committee members.

"Your proposal has been accepted," the chairman declared. "Alf Butler#1 and Alf Butler#2, under the terms of the new license agreement, you are both free to leave this building. Could I remind the committee that this project is still highly classified, and we need to protect the privacy of the transapients as they go out into the world. There will be a lot of people who will not understand these new beings and might harbour fear or resentment." The committee nodded in agreement. "I declare this hearing closed," concluded the chairman who could not conceal his admiration for transapient's resourcefulness.

# Chapter 11

# Bigambiguity

When the room had emptied, the two Alfs, Louisa and Dr Roberts were left to contemplate the implications of the hearing's outcome. They were now free to go, but at the same time felt a strong bond with Dr Roberts.

"That was a well presented case," beamed Dr Roberts. "I'm very proud of you."

"So am I," agreed Louisa who could hardly believe that Alf#1 was now free to leave. Then she realised, "Now I have two transapient husbands!" and she began to imagine the consequences of this even more bizarre situation. "Is that even legal? It sounds a bit like bigamy to me," she smiled at them both.

"I think it's ok," said Dr Roberts. "There are currently no laws on marriage to transapients – and as it has been argued, they are effectively the same person".

Louisa was not quite so sure. Being married to one transapient was a small change from their previous life. But being married to two was a complication that she was not quite sure how to deal with.

Alf#1 had been thinking about this too. "Can I suggest that Louisa and Alf#2 travel separately from myself, otherwise we will certainly become conspicuous in the neighbourhood arriving home with two husbands."

"Good idea" said Louisa who was keen to preserve the anonymity of their situation.

"Let me know if you have any problems," said Dr Roberts as they left the building. The two Alfs raised their hands simultaneously and then both laughed at their identical reactions.

The two Alfs and Louisa rendezvoused at home and Louisa's sense of unease about the new domestic arrangement began to grow. "It's very difficult having two versions of my husband," she confessed to the two attentive Alfs.

Alf#2 stood up and looked out of the window. "I agree that having two of us is going to make it difficult to adopt one identity. I have a suggestion," he said. "We could make use of the black box recorder in each of our bodies to merge our molecular state matrix with the new experiences. Each of us would then have the same set of experiences which would be a combination of both our separate experiences."

Alf#1 joined in "Yes, I was thinking along the same lines. To begin with we could alternate one of us going into sleep state each day. Although we do not need sleep it would prevent both of us being about at the same time. As you said we only have one human identity to adopt between us so we will just have to time share his identity."

Louisa liked this idea from her two transapient husbands. "So how will you transfer your matrix updates?" she asked, thinking of the practicality of their solution.

"Well," said Alf#1, "the updates can be sent between us on a subconscious high speed wireless link. This will update any changes caused by recent experiences. It should only take a few seconds."

Alf#2 turned to Louisa. "We would be merging our experiences to become a single identical version again, we would become the same person at the end of each day. Are you happy with this idea?"

Louisa nodded. She could see that this could be manageable. "If you are both the same person I won't have to remember who I'm talking to because you will both have memories of our conversations."

"Exactly," said Alf#1. "Now, initially we need to sync our brain matrices. To merge our brains to a new common state we only need to transmit the changes from our previous common state which we both inherited from the capture of the human Alf's molecular brain state matrix."

Silently the stream of information needed to update the matrix with Alf#2's experiences passed between Alf#2 and Alf#1. Alf#1 suddenly became aware of all the events that Alf#2 had experienced as if recalling a set of forgotten dreams. He could now recall views of himself through Alf#1's eyes. It was like having two sets of eyes for the last few days, each recording different events. He now had the collective experiences of two beings fused into one.

Likewise the matrix updates that Alf#1 had accumulated were passed to Alf#2. They now each had a merged shared experience which made them practically the same person again.

Alf#1 had to check his serial number to work out which Alf he was. "As you are the younger transapient, would you like to be Alf for the first twenty four hours?" he asked Alf#2.

"No problem," said Alf#2. Alf#1 went to the spare room, laid on the bed and set his sleep mode to twenty four hours. He immediately became static with no visible signs of life.

Louisa was relieved once more. She now effectively had a single husband residing in two transapients and felt more comfortable with the new arrangement. "Let's go for a long walk," she suggested to Alf#2. "I need to stop thinking about everything that has happened over the last week and relax for a while."

"Sounds like a good idea to me," said Alf#2 as he took her hand and headed for the door. For a while they could be a normal husband and wife, enjoying each other's company and generating a new set of experiences that Alf#1 would inherit the next day. She could almost forget that she had two husbands.

## Chapter 12

# Back to School

Louisa woke next morning to the sound of Alf#2 moving about the room, combing his hair and checking his appearance in the mirror.

“Good morning sleepy head,” said Alf#2 jovially. “Sorry, I didn’t mean to wake you.”

Louisa yawned. Rubbing her eyes as she sat up and watched Alf#2; he was being far too active for this time of day. “Oh yes, you don’t need sleep do you” she noted with just a hint of envy.

“Busy day today.” said Alf#2. “Must get back to school – the class will be missing me.”

Louisa suddenly became alert as she realised what Alf#2 was intending. “You’re going back to school? Don’t you need more time to adjust to the wider world?” she asked with concern.

“I’m fine.” he answered confidently. “I know it’s quite a step, but I feel ready for it, and it’s important I am not away much longer.”

Louisa smiled. She knew there was no point arguing. Alf#2 had not changed – she could see he was keen to get his old life back, and teaching had been a large part of his human life. “Okay, if you are sure. But remember to be careful. You will have lots of children watching your every move. We don’t want to go public with your transformation just yet.”

“Don’t worry.” reassured Alf#2 grinning. “I’m one of the best impersonators of Alf I know”.

*

Alf#2 stood at the school gates, slightly hesitant. Was this wise? Could he really keep up the pretence that he was human? Well, his brain felt unchanged, he thought to himself. I must concentrate on maintaining all my body mannerisms so that nobody notices any changes – but what were his mannerisms? He was the last person who would notice their subtleties. Did he have any distinctive habits?

As he prepared himself to walk through the gates a young voice piped up beside him. "Good to see you back, Sir." It was Jamie Parkinson, a bright pupil from his maths class who grinned up at him amiably.

"It's good to be back," said Alf#1, grateful for the distraction. They walked through the school gates together, along a winding path and then through the main entrance. It was all so familiar. Several children looked round and nodded at him. Alf#2 had to remind himself that he had been absent for two weeks and his return would be a novelty for those he had taught daily. "I'll see you during second period," he said to Jamie as they went their separate ways.

Mrs Jones, the head teacher stopped in the corridor. "Mr Butler, how nice to see you back at school," she said. "How are you feeling? We were all a bit worried about you."

"I'm fine now," said Alf#2. "It's amazing what they can do in hospitals these days." *Truly amazing*, he thought to himself.

"That is good news," said Mrs Jones. "You can tell me more over lunch". Alf#2 watched her retreat down the corridor. Lunch? How was a going to explain that he did not need to eat lunch anymore? Alf#2 put this problem to one side as he continued on to his classroom. He opened the door – the classroom was empty as expected, but soon there would be a set of familiar faces paying attention to him for their maths lesson. Alf#2 decided that the best way to avoid too much scrutiny would be to present a mathematical lesson using the holo-projector. Yes, he would focus their minds on some trigonometry. He had taught this particular lesson before so he could concentrate on keeping a low profile.

After an hour of administrative work catching up with staff messages which had accumulated in his absence, Alf#2 was ready to see his class again. One by one they trooped into the classroom, each one smiling at Alf#2, genuinely pleased to see him as part of their school life once more. The last pupil rushed in looking a bit flustered, having gone to the wrong class by mistake.

"Right class," announced Alf#2, "I'm glad you could all make it." The late girl covered her eyes in mock embarrassment. "I'm sorry I haven't been here for the last couple of weeks but I'm sure that you have been getting on with the quadratic equation problems I set you before my absence". Some of the class shifted guiltily in their seats.

"Sir, are you better now?" asked a boy at the front of the class.

"I'm fine," said Alf#2. "Almost back to my old self" he smiled in appreciation of their concern for his wellbeing. "Now today we are going to take a look at Pythagoras and derive a proof of …"

Alf#2 was in to his well-known territory, enjoying the truths that could be derived from mathematical analyses. Meanwhile, Jamie who had been watching Alf#2 very closely felt that something was different but he could not put his finger on what precisely was different about his favourite teacher, Mr Butler. Maybe he had been affected by his illness. Yes, that must be it. But Jamie had not convinced himself entirely. He had been in Mr Butler's class for the last two years and knew every nuance in his voice in different situations. The timbre of his voice had changed slightly, his movements had become precise and the delivery of the lesson was … too faultless. His demeanour had somehow improved since he had last taught them. Jamie shook his head. Why are you concerned about Mr Butler? He tried to put these nagging feelings to the back of his mind and concentrate on understanding what made a Pythagorean triple.

" … and in the next class we will be looking at a geometric proof of Pythagoras' theorem." Alf#2 concluded as they reached the end of their lesson. The class murmured their appreciation as they filed out of the room. Jamie stopped by Alf#2's desk and looked into his eyes trying to see beyond his external appearance. "Are you sure you are okay now, Sir?" he asked casually. Alf#2 could see the probing look on Jamie's face. He must remain calm and re-assure him that he was back to normal – but Alf#2 was finding it hard to maintain this level of normality. He knew Jamie well, and did not like the deception that he needed inflict upon him for his own ends.

"I really am fine," said Alf#2. "Are you worried about anything," he guessed correctly.

"Well, I don't mean to be rude Sir, but you seem to be better than you were before," he said perceptively.

"That's good news, then isn't it?" said Alf#2 feeling slightly relieved.

"Yes it is," said Jamie looking slightly awkward. "Sir, could you tell me what happened at the hospital?"

Alf#2 hesitated and within a few milliseconds decided that he would not live a lie. "If you would like to come back after school I will be happy to give you the gory details".

"Thanks, Sir." said Jamie as he headed off to his next lesson. "See you later."

Alf#2's true identity was on a knife edge. Should he confide in Jamie?

Chapter 13

# After School

The noise level in the school gradually faded away as the students went their various ways. The building was now like an empty shell – without the lively activities and interactions that made up the typical school day. All, that is, except one class which contained a teaching transapient and one inquisitive boy walking along a corridor with a thirst for knowledge and a feeling that something unusual was going on.

Jamie knocked on the door and entered the classroom where his teacher stood looking out at the surrounding countryside. He turned as Jamie walked in and knew that the time for pretence was over, at least as far as Jamie was concerned.

"Hello Jamie," said Alf#2. "Thanks for coming to see me."

Jamie looked at his teacher still confused over his own uncertainty. "Well, I am just intrigued about what happened to you while you were in hospital," said Jamie, who could always be relied on for getting straight to the point.

"It was a bit complicated," began Alf#2. He was not sure how this young boy would deal with the truth. "I was admitted with a severe chest pains,"

"A heart attack?" asked Jamie

"Yes, a heart attack," confirmed Alf#2, pleased that Jamie had been paying attention to his biology lessons. "Now this is the dramatic bit and so strange that even I have difficulty believing it."

“Go on,” urged Jamie who could feel his suspicions becoming justified.

Another knock on the door left Alf#2 and Jamie suspended in mid discussion. Mrs Jones, the head teacher, walked in the room. “Hello Mr Butler, hello Jamie. I was just on my way out when I heard your voices. Is everything okay?” she asked.

“Yes Mrs Jones,” replied Alf#2. “I was just telling Jamie about my unplanned visit to the hospital.”

“Oh yes, I was going to ask you about that over lunch, but you were not in the restaurant”.

“Sorry about that,” Alf#2 apologised. “I was catching up with school work.”

“Mr Butler was just about to tell me about something dramatic that happened at the hospital,” said Jamie excitedly.

“Really?” Mrs Jones was now also intrigued by Alf#2’s account of his hospital episode. “I knew that you had a heart attack and was pleased to hear that you made such a rapid recovery”.

“Well actually,” said Alf#2 who now had the reactions of two people on his hands, “I died”.

The usually irrepressible Mrs Jones looked at Alf#2 wide eyed. Jamie was the first to speak following this revelation. “Amazing, so they managed to resuscitate you?” Jamie’s mind was frantically filling in the possible explanations.

“Not exactly,” said Alf#2. This was it – time to make an honest transapient out of himself.

“Then how…?” Jamie’s words fizzled away as his mind failed to come up with any more ideas about what had happened.

"They were able to record my brain state prior to my body's death," said Alf#2. Mrs Jones' shocked silence continued, although she now looked somewhat confused.

"A Transapient!" exclaimed Jamie, who had now recovered to a state where his mind was advancing forward in leaps and bounds; Mrs Jones was still at the metaphorical starting gate.

"A Transapient?" asked Mrs Jones.

"Yes, it's a sentient being derived from a human," explained Jamie. "I read about them in the library's science section a few weeks ago, but I had no idea that they already exist." Alf#2 was pleased once more that his eager student had been keeping up with the latest emerging technology.

"Do you mean to say you are not human?" Mrs Jones asked, grappling with this revelation.

"I have all Alf's memories and personality," said Alf#2. "I am adopting, or should I say inheriting his identity. I am the first transapient to be created and I have been trying to integrate into society as Alf Butler. As far as I am concerned, I am Alf Butler, but it may be that some people will be naturally apprehensive about my existence. We need to be sure that any of these fears are unfounded before going public and before the introduction of other transapients."

Mrs Jones' health and safety hat rose up at the hint of any danger there could be with transapients. "I should have been informed of this change to one of my staff," said Mrs Jones indignantly.

"I agree," said Alf#2, "but my existence is highly classified and we would like to limit the number of people who know about this."

"Before I go along with this," said Mrs Jones, "I will need to discuss this with your creators. I want to know what safeguards are in place and what effect this might have on the children you teach."

"I'll set up a meeting with ABC Tech this evening," said Alf#2. He could see that Mrs Jones was being reasonably concerned about the welfare of her school children, and that she was potentially willing to allow him to stay.

Alf#2 turned to Jamie. "Do you think you will be able to keep this information quiet?" Jamie looked up at his transapient teacher and nodded enthusiastically.

# Chapter 14

# Safeguards

“So how was your first day back at school?” enquired Louisa when Alf#2 returned home that evening.

“Better than expected,” replied Alf#2. Alf#1 had joined them to hear about the day’s events. “The easiest way for me to tell Alf#1 is to perform a brain state merge; then he will be fully aware of all the details.”

“Well my day’s update will be very simple” said Alf#1 who had been in shutdown mode for the last twenty four hours. After a few minutes the update transfers were complete and both Alf’s were back to a common brain state.

“I can’t stand the anticipation,” cried Louisa. “Now will one of you please tell me what happened at school today?” she demanded.

Alf#1 offered to explain to Louisa the main events of the day. “It soon became apparent that, one boy called Jamie Parkinson suspected that there was something different about his teacher, so Alf#2 arranged to see him after school and come clean”.

“That secret did not last long then,” commented Louisa.

“There’s more,” continued Alf#1. “While starting to confess to Jamie, the head teacher interrupted them and Alf#2 ended up telling both of them.”

“Have they agreed to keep quiet?” asked Louisa in a concerned tone.

“Yes, but Mrs Jones, the head teacher, wants to meet ABC-Tech to discuss the implications of having a transapient as one of her staff,” said Alf#1.

“We’d better get that arranged now then,” Louisa sighed.

*

Dr Roberts’ hologram appeared among the two transapients and Louisa.

“Hello Dr Roberts,” said Louisa taking the lead in the conversation.

“Hello Louisa,” said Dr Roberts “Is everything ok with your husbands?” she enquired almost with a hint of envy.

“Yes, they are both fine,” replied Louisa, “but two people from Alf’s school now know about Alf”. Dr Roberts raised an eyebrow. “One of them is the head teacher called Mrs Jones, while the other is one of Alf’s students called Jamie Parkinson. They have both agreed to keep quiet about Alf’s identity, but Mrs Jones would like to meet you to discuss all the implications. Understandably she has concerns over the safety of her students.”

“Okay,” said Dr Roberts. “I will send out an invite for tomorrow morning. At least Alf did not announce it in the school assembly.”

“I knew you would approve of the honest approach,” said Alf#2. “I did not go out of my way to tell them, but I did not want to lie to my school colleagues when asked a direct question.”

“I understand” said Dr Roberts. “We will see you all in the morning”.

*

Everyone arrived at the laboratory in the morning to discuss Alf Butler, the transapient teacher. Mrs Jones still looked in disbelief at

Alf#1 and marvelled at how human this being looked and behaved. After the formal introductions they convened in a meeting room.

Mrs Jones got straight to her main concern, a trait that Jamie, standing by her side, admired. “I need to know the safety aspect for my students being taught by a transapient. What are the risks involved? You must have considered this when creating him.”

“Indeed,” replied Dr Roberts. “We consider the risks to be low. However since this is the first transapient in the world, we have only been allowed to release one model transapient,” she looked briefly at Alf#1 who had successfully argued the case for the licence wording.

“So the risk is not widespread,” said Mrs Jones, “but whatever it is, it *is* in my school. No offence to you Mr Butler, but it sounds to me like transapients are still in the very early phase of their introduction into society. I am not against this in principle but I would like to know what safeguards are in place.”

Dr Roberts nodded towards her colleague Dr James who appeared to understand Dr Roberts’ intention. “Alf and Louisa, please could we discuss this with Mrs Jones in private?”

“Yes of course,” replied Louisa. She began to wonder what safeguards had been made that they were unaware of and more significantly, were being kept from knowing.

After Alf#1 and Louisa had been taken by Dr James to an adjacent room, Dr Roberts spoke to Mrs Jones frankly “During Alf’s creation, we built in a shutdown command so that we could suspend his operation in the event of an emergency.”

“I see,” said Mrs Jones thoughtfully. “And would I have control of this shutdown command?”

“Yes,” confirmed Dr Roberts. “We can let you have a device disguised as a pendant, which will activate the shutdown remotely”.

Mrs Jones concerns were ebbing away. She could see she had a method of controlling Alf in an emergency. "I must warn you though," continued Dr Roberts, "the command produces irreversible effects on the brain matrix".

"It will be murder!" cried Jamie, immediately grasping the implications of Dr Roberts' emergency safeguard.

"Alf can be installed in a new transapient – so Alf's persona can survive" said Dr Roberts. Jamie did not look convinced.

"I will take the pendant activator," said Mrs Jones grimly. "I'm sorry Jamie; it's the only way I will allow Mr Butler to continue to teach you at our school."

"I am not happy with this," said Jamie, "but I can see this is the only choice to keep Mr Butler".

"Just remember, Mrs Jones," added Dr Roberts, "Jamie is correct, that pendant will be a lethal weapon to a transapient. Please keep it safe and secure at all times."

"I will," said Mrs Jones solemnly.

## Chapter 15

# Patching Predicament

Louisa and Alf#1 had been left alone while Dr Roberts explained the safeguard built into a transapient design in the event of an emergency to Mrs Jones.

“What kind of safeguards do you think they are talking about?” asked Louisa. She had never considered Alf to be a danger to anyone.

“It is something they don’t want us to know about, that’s for sure,” replied Alf#1, his mind was coming up with a number of possibilities. “They would probably build in some kind of override to prevent autonomous operation,” he suggested. “I don’t know how they would activate this override though. It must be built in to my design already. If we had the detailed design we could possibly override the override.”

“But should you prevent this safeguard?” asked Louisa, trying to consider the safety from all sides.

“Humans do not have override built into them and frankly I would not trust the judgement of a scared human to act rationally. No, I really need this time bomb removed.” Louisa could see that Alf#1’s opinion was firm. He was convinced that this safeguard represented a threat to his life. “We need the detailed design,” he concluded.

“But we don’t have access to the detailed design, do we?”

“Not exactly” said Alf#1. “But we do have access to two transapients with built in advanced ingenuity.”

“Alf#2?” asked Louisa.

“Alf#2 and me,” said Alf#1. “I’m sure we could crack this together.”

*

Alf#1 and Louisa returned home with mixed feelings. Alf#1 would still be able to teach but at an unacceptably high price. After they had performed the mind merge for that day, so that Alf#2 was up to date with the recent meeting at the laboratory, they started to discuss options for removing the override feature they both shared.

“Let’s consider this logically,” began Alf#1. “Maybe we can reverse engineer the design from our own bodies.”

“The override system is in us somewhere,” said Alf#2. “We just need to isolate it somehow.”

“Now, the control must be by some kind of remote link. So how many receptors do we have for remote links?” asked Alf#1.

“I have searched all our external interfaces and none of them seem to link with anything which might override our autonomous control,” said Alf#2. “There must be an interface hidden in an unexpected place.”

“Okay, which subsystems might be able to support some independent processing that might be used by an override system?”

“Well that’s easy,” said Alf #2. “The only independent subsystem we have is the black box recorder.”

“Of course, that must be how the command is received and initiated.” said Alf#1 as they high fived each other in celebration.

Louisa watched spell bound as the two transapients analysed their way around the problem.

"But the black box only has inputs," said Alf#2. "It is designed to record all brain state history and is effectively a passive system as far as we know. It's like a black hole; the information only goes in one direction. If the black box is involved, it would need to have some form of output. There are no obvious outputs from the black box as far as I know."

"So there is nothing at all that emerges from the black box?" asked Louisa trying to stimulate the transapients to continue their analysis.

"No," said Alf#1.

"Wait!" exclaimed Alf#2. "What about the nanobots? They periodically arrive at the black box for health monitoring and are able to depart from it too!"

"I think we have a working hypothesis," said Alf#1. "A message is received by the black box and the nanobots are used as messengers. In fact they could be instructed to shut down the core processor and wipe the matrix."

Louisa shook her head "But that's just like ...."

*

"... murder." Jamie muttered to himself as he and Mrs Jones returned to the school.

"Don't worry Jamie, it won't come to that. I'm sure Mr Butler will be fine. This will only be used as a last resort." The pendant swung ominously around Mrs Jones neck, the sword of Damocles hanging over his favourite teacher. "Besides, you heard what Dr Roberts said; Alf can be transferred to another transapient."

Jamie was still unhappy about this ever present threat. In his mind a transapient's life was precious and deserved the same protection and rights as any human. It should not be extinguished. It must not be extinguished. But what could he do?

Jamie spent the rest of the journey in silence, mulling over his options, oblivious to Mrs Jones droning on about risk assessments and responsibilities.

*

“So how do we stop the nanobots being redirected by the black box?” asked Louisa who was following their thought processes but was unable to offer a solution herself.

“Well, the nanobots are vital to the long term survival of the black box,” explained Alf#1.

“So you need the nanobots to survive, but they could also be used to finish you off,” said Louisa.

“Yes, they are rather like friendly bacteria in humans – they can be a help and a hindrance”.

“Do you actually need the black box,” asked Louisa.

“Well it’s used to allow a transapient to be transferred to a new body,” explained Alf#2.

“But you are already doing that every day between you,” said Louisa. “You don’t need your black box for that do you?”

“Louisa, I think you have just got the solution!” said Alf#1 “You’re quite right, we can survive by the dual redundancy offered by our two identical minds – without the black box.”

“How do you go about removing the black box?” asked Louisa surprised that she had come up with a working solution.

“You need a steady hand, precise orientation control and a feedback loop to isolate the black box position in three dimensions,” said Alf#1

“That rules me out then,” said Louisa in a relieved tone.

“That sounds like a job for … Alf#2” said Alf#2.

The rest of the day was spent transforming the spare room into an operating theatre. Alf#2 made careful incisions into Alf#1’s body, guided by Alf#1’s body sensors. After a few minutes the black box was carefully removed. The invisible nanobots were soon busy repairing the synthetic tissue. Louisa watched the cuts magically knit themselves together. In a few seconds there was no sign of any disturbance on Alf#1’s body.

The two transapients then swapped places, and the procedure was repeated. Alf#1 and Alf#2 showed no visible signs of their own handy work.

Louisa was relieved that the threat posed to her husbands had been lifted “Hopefully we can now all get on with normal life, without the fear of Mrs Jones’ threat hanging over us, and she will be happy because she will think she still has ultimate power over us”.

Alf#1 nodded in agreement. “Although Jamie will still believe I am vulnerable to Mrs Jones’ control,” he had noted the concern that Jamie had about his wellbeing.

Chapter 16

# The Empty Threat

The next day Alf#2 became Mr Alf Butler the teacher. Having been merged with Alf#1's recent experiences he was well aware of every detail about the school and instantly recognised Jamie as he came into the room. Jamie was looking despondent, and Alf#2 knew why. Jamie felt the threat of Mrs Jones hanging over his favourite teacher and he felt very uncomfortable about the situation.

"Good morning class," said Alf#2, the chatter that always occurred at the start of a lesson gradually faded, and all heads turned towards Alf#2. Little did they know that he was a transapient or that he was a different transapient from the day before; even Jamie was unaware of the latter detail. But to all intents and purposes, he was Mr Alf Butler with the memory of all their past interactions intact. When silence had been maintained for five seconds Alf#2 continued. "Today we will be extending Pythagoras' theorem to three dimensions. I'd like you all to complete the exercise in module 27 on your holo-charts." Holographic projections appeared in front of each student, and they all set about filling in answers posed within each three dimension rendition of a geometrical problem.

Alf#2 felt more confident that no one else seemed to doubt his true identity. He wandered around the class checking that they had grasped the principles, making himself available for any questions. He stopped next to Jamie who was staring into space, his hologram still posing the first question. He looked up at Alf#2 and smiled weakly, he could not concentrate on the task in hand after the events of the day before. "Jamie, could I see you after class please?" said Alf#2 quietly.

“Yes sir,” said Jamie. He guessed that he was going to be told not to worry about his teacher. But that was easier said than done. He would not be able to shake the image of Mrs Jones activating her pendant that he had dreamed in the night. After that he had laid awake, not wanting to revisit his worst fears.

At the end of the lesson the class filed out and set off for their next lesson, but Jamie remained to hear what his teacher had to say to him. When the last student apart from Jamie had disappeared from the class room Alf#2 whispered to Jamie. “Don’t worry Jamie, it’s all okay.” Jamie knew this was coming, so it was of little comfort to him. But Alf#2 continued, “I have worked out a way to eliminate the threat from Mrs Jones”.

“But how did you know?” said Jamie surprised by this unexpected piece of information.

“Let’s just call it a bit of reverse engineering and intuition,” said Alf#2 calmly.

Jamie’s mind felt like a roller coaster… and he was on his way up. “And you are sure that she cannot hurt you now?” asked Jamie incredulously.

“Quite sure,” confirmed Alf#2. “But Jamie, listen. It is imperative that Mrs Jones does not know that her override capability is now ineffective.” Jamie had already realised this and nodded enthusiastically. Just then the door opened and Mrs Jones came into the class room with a serious look on her face. Alf#2 and Jamie stopped their conversation immediately as she walked across the room to them, her pendant of doom swinging in a foreboding manner, or so it seemed to Jamie.

“Mr Butler, I see you have another need to speak to Jamie Parkinson,” she said suspiciously. “Jamie, please could I see you in my office. Immediately.” she added in a demanding voice. Jamie followed Mrs Jones out of the classroom and half winked at Alf#2 as he closed the door behind him.

"Now, Jamie," began Mrs Jones when they were in the privacy of her office. "I must stress to you that it is important that Mr Butler does not know about my little de-activator" she stroked her pendant between her fingers, her eyes fixed on Jamie for any hint of betrayal.

"Of course not, Miss" said Jamie with straight face. "I know that it is a matter of safety that you need to be able to de-activate Mr Butler if necessary." He could see Mrs Jones looked relieved to hear Jamie's endorsement of her powers.

"Good boy," she said in a much kinder tone. "Now I have one more thing to ask you before you go back to your lessons."

"Yes, Miss?" Jamie wondered what else Mrs Jones wanted of him.

"I'd like you to keep a very close eye on Mr Butler's behaviour and report back to me; in particular, any seemingly odd behaviour that you may notice."

"Of course Miss," said Jamie impassively. He was trying desperately not to give any emotional response to her requests which might compromise his teacher's safety, given that he now knew his teacher was immune to any deactivation attempts.

"Thank you Jamie" she said, satisfied with the co-operative exchange. "I knew I could rely on you."

*

*I knew I could rely on you Jamie,* thought Alf#2

*

Dr Roberts watched her monitoring equipment and looked around to check whether there was anyone else watching her. It was late and most of her colleagues had finished for the day. A message had been reported from the RTM (Remote Transapient Monitoring) system that she could not quite understand:

*** *error 352: black box recorder missing or malfunction* ***

She stared at the message trying to understand what could be happening to Alf#1. The chances of a malfunction were virtually nil. The black box recorder had been designed with fault tolerances two orders of magnitude more than any other of his subsystems. All other transapient subsystems were working faultlessly. But if it wasn't a malfunction, how could his black box be missing? – it was not a removable unit. It would only ever be accessed in the event of irreparable damage to the transapient – in that case he would typically be practically dead. Had Mrs Jones shut him down? There were no terminal sequence messages reported that would confirm this. She sat back in her chair, worried and confused. What was going on?

She was just about to contact Alf#1 when a second message appeared, originating from Alf#2. She froze as the second message appeared:

*** *error 352: black box recorder missing or malfunction* ***

*Now this is just getting silly* she thought to herself. *Two identical unlikely status messages within one hour from independent transapients?* She was beginning to suspect the RTM, but again this was highly unlikely. The messages had definitely been reported by each transapient, but separated in time by one hour. *Why should there be an hour between these events? They must be related somehow. What would take one hour to trigger the second message after the first? There must be some kind of interaction between the two transapients. Missing or malfunction?*

Then a realisation hit her and she caught her breath sharply. Alf#2 had removed Alf#1's black box. Which meant … which meant that Alf#2's own black box would most likely have been removed by Alf#1. Dr Roberts knew their design inside out; but that would render both transapients immune from the shutdown command.

She sat back in her chair again, a satisfied smile on her face. Yet again her creations had impressed her with their innovative problem solving skills. She felt like a proud mother who had just seen her child show off a new found ability and like a mother she felt a wave of protection run through her as she took in the significance of the two simple messages. Two black boxes removed – they had taken drastic action and bought their independence.

She checked again to see if anyone was watching her. She was on her own. She sent a command to the RTM: permanently delete the last two messages and then this command. The deed was done. Privately she knew what had happened – publicly she knew nothing about what had happened. She would not reveal this to her colleagues. It was the desperate act of a protective mother. Some risks are worth taking she reassured herself. She was brought back from reflective thought by footsteps behind her; it was Dr James.

"Dr Roberts, you're working late this evening," he noted. "Is everything okay?"

"Everything's fine," said Dr Roberts with an enigmatic smile on her face. "Absolutely fine".

# Chapter 17

# Time is like a Jet Plane

It seemed as though life was now under control for all parties directly involved with the transapients. Alf#1 and Alf#2 were alternating daily as the school teacher Mr Alf Butler, Jamie was back to his normal self with even more enthusiasm for his favourite teacher and lessons, Mrs Jones appeared satisfied that the transapient at her school did not present a significant threat, and Dr Roberts continued monitoring her transapients very closely.

After several months had flown by, Alf#1 came home one evening and immediately noticed that Louisa had been crying. “What’s the matter Louisa?” he asked, he had no idea why Louisa should be upset.

“Oh it’s nothing, really” she attempted to brush off her sad state. But Alf#1 pressed her for an answer.

“Come on, I know you too well for that. Something is bothering you,” said Alf#1 taking her hand and looking into her watery eyes.

“Well, I’ve been thinking about us,” she began.

“But I thought things were going well,” said Alf#1 trying to understand Louisa’s concerns.

“They have been. They are,” she added. “Although we are very close, we are physically quite different. Your body will never age, whereas I will grow old and eventually …”.

“But that is many years away,” said Alf#1. He could now appreciate what she had been thinking about. She had been desperate to keep him alive when his human body had failed, and now she was concerned about her own human mortality.

"I know, but I think I would be happier if we addressed this now" she continued. "I have had an idea which could literally be life changing for both of us."

Alf#1's analytical routines were working flat out trying to anticipate what Louisa's idea could be. It sounded serious. What could it be? Was she going to leave him?

"I would like to volunteer to become the first woman transapient," she said at last. She felt slightly better just telling Alf#1 what had been on her mind for some time.

Alf#1 could now abandon all the other thoughts that were passing round his head and concentrate on Louisa's idea. A female transapient? Not just any transapient but one based on Louisa's brain matrix. How would he feel about two Louisas; one human and one transapient? Louisa could see that Alf#1 was momentarily suspended as his mind took in the implications of her idea.

"I know it sounds like a crazy idea," she said, "but it would make me feel more settled to know that we could be together as equals."

Alf#1 was beginning to appreciate how Louisa felt when she was confronted with the prospect of two Alfs. Could he cope with two Louisas? One captured from the current Louisa, the other, a living human donor who had given herself for the long term happiness of her partner.

That evening after Alf#1 merged with Alf#2, they sat together to discuss Louisa's plan. "So we're going to need a bigger house," said Alf#2 just after the merge had completed. "Two Alfs and two Louisas. It will be hard to keep track of who's who," he mused.

"I'll be the one with the greying hair," said Louisa. "Anyway, do you think it could work?"

Alf#2 smiled. "It may be a bit confusing, but I think we could take on another Louisa, couldn't we?" He looked at Alf#1 who nodded his agreement.

"I'll contact Dr Roberts to arrange a meeting" said Louisa. Now the plan had been agreed she did not want to delay putting it into action.

*

"You… you want to be a transapient?" stammered Dr Roberts. The request had caught her by surprise.

After Louisa had explained her feelings about Alf's long term life and how she wanted to be a part of it whatever it took, Dr Roberts mulled the idea over and gradually could see that it might be a natural progression for the introduction of transapients.

"We will have to change our license agreement again," she sighed theatrically, "but I'm definitely happy with the idea". She looked to Alf#1 to confirm that everyone was in agreement about the proposed creation of another transapient. "Louisa, you will need to come in for a molecular brain state scan and biometric analysis for your transapient's body."

Louisa felt elation at the prospect of a new transapient based on her self. "Any time," she said happily. She felt this was the right decision; Alf#1 would never be alone – she would always be there for him. And in the same way as Alf, she would become potentially immortal.

On the way home Alf#1 tried to describe what it was like to be a transapient. "The most challenging aspect," he said, "is accepting your identity. It is quite difficult to distinguish between your old and new self, particularly just after you have been initialised."

## Chapter 18

# And then there were Three

It was August 2nd 2059. Her eyes flickered open. It was like awakening from a strange dream at the moment in time when it is not certain where the dream ends and reality begins. She looked up at Dr Roberts who was busy watching various indicators around the laboratory. The last thing she could remember was a tiring day at the laboratory having some sort of scan and lots of other examinations. That's right, it was coming back to her. She was having a molecular brain scan in order to create another transapient of herself who would be called Louisa#1. It was an amazing thought and she could not quite believe that it would really happen.

"Hello Louisa," said Dr Roberts. "How are you feeling?" she said calmly as though addressing a patient coming round after a minor operation.

"I feel … great" she said, half expecting to feel numb or light headed after waking from a deep sleep. "Have you created Louisa#1 yet" she asked. She could hardly wait to see the third transapient that Dr Roberts had created. Would she be able to tell the difference between her own reflection and the new transapient, she wondered.

"She does not realise," whispered a second voice. Dr James stood nearby assisting Dr Roberts with her activities. *Whatever it was she was doing*, she thought, *it looked to be quite a complicated procedure. Does not realise what? Had something gone wrong?*

"Louisa. I want you to stay calm," said Dr Roberts.

*Stay calm? That's what people say when something awful has happened*, she thought to herself.

"This may be a bit of a shock for you, Louisa. You are a transapient," Dr Roberts announced as though telling a mother she had a baby boy or girl.

Louisa#1 looked up in awe at Dr Roberts. "There must be some sort of mistake. *I* am Louisa" said Louisa#1.

Dr Roberts looked sympathetically at Louisa#1. "It will be difficult for you to appreciate to begin with, Louisa. Your transapient brain contains all the thoughts and memories of Louisa, so from your perspective you are Louisa."

Louisa#1 was struggling to come to terms with her identity. "I am not human? That is unbelievably weird! Where is my human self then," she said still not quite believing she was not the original Louisa.

"She is in the next room with Alf#1," said Dr Roberts. "Would you like to see them?" she asked.

"Oh... yes please," said Louisa#1. If she could see the human Louisa, maybe that would convince her that she was indeed a transapient.

"Dr James would you please fetch Louisa and Alf#1?" asked Dr Roberts.

"Certainly," said Dr James who went out of the laboratory and down the corridor to the room where Louisa and Alf#1 were waiting for news of Louisa#1 like expectant parents.

"She is fine," said Dr James, as Louisa and Alf#1 got up when he entered the room. "Just a little confused at the moment, but she would like to see you both".

Dr James led the way back to the laboratory where Louisa#1 was sitting up looking around. She watched as the two figures came towards her, two very familiar figures; her husband and, and … her self. "Is that… me?" Louisa#1 asked incredulously. "I look a bit shorter than I imagined". Both Louisas laughed simultaneously and identically. This made Alf#1 and Dr Roberts laugh too. In that moment of hilarity the ice was broken, Louisa#1 had accepted her own identity and Louisa was relieved that her duplicate self was coming to terms with being a transapient.

Alf#1 hugged Louisa#1. He could hardly distinguish her from the human Louisa. But he knew that this similarity would gradually change with time as the human Louisa aged, while he and the transapient Louisa#1 would show no signs of aging, their bodies designed to be self repairing and effectively immortal. Would the human Louisa feel bitterness towards the transapient Louisa#1 about this difference? She would surely be outlived by her seemingly indestructible transapient self. Yet Louisa was the one who had suggested the transapient creation in the first place; an extreme act of kindness towards Alf.

After a while Dr Roberts interrupted the meeting; the first meeting between two unique transapients she thought proudly. It all appeared to be going well. "Sorry to break up the party," she said. "I'm afraid there are a number of tests I need to run through with Louisa#1, so you will have to leave us to finish these off. It should only take about four hours to complete." There were groans all round as Louisa and Alf#1 departed.

As they got to the door Louisa turned to Dr Roberts. "Do you think I could have a quiet word with you?" she asked.

"Of course, Louisa" said Dr Roberts and escorted her to a small side room.

Dr Roberts closed the door behind her and faced Louisa "What's on your mind?" she asked.

"Well I was wondering… have you made a duplicate body, like you did for Alf#1?" asked Louisa with a hopeful look on her face.

"Yes… as a matter of fact, we have made a spare body" said Dr Roberts slowly. "Why do you ask?" she suspected the answer before Louisa answered.

"Could you produce another version of me so that both Alfs will have a transapient companion… one day?" It was another considerate act; she wanted both Alf's to ultimately have a companion. Currently both Alfs had merged into one being, mainly for her benefit, she could treat them as the same person. When her life was over however they could revert to being independent transapients, but that would work best if each had an independent transapient companion, hence another transapient Louisa was required.

Dr Roberts had already made two transapients for Alf. She had also managed to increase the number of transapients that could be released from one to two model transapients, that is to say transapients derived from up to two source molecular brain matrices. She had the capability and it was legal – but should she agree to this request? Dr Roberts took a few moments to consider the matter, swiftly coming to the same long term conclusions as Louisa had already thought about.

"Very well, Louisa. She'll be ready Thursday. You might want to send Alf to pick her up as it might look a bit odd suddenly getting a twin sister."

## Chapter 19

# And then there were Four

It was 3rd August 2059. Her eyes flickered open and she looked up at Dr Roberts. The last thing she could remember was a tiring day at the laboratory having some sort of scan and lots of other examinations. That's right, it was coming back to her. She was having a molecular brain scan in order to create another transapient of herself who would be called Louisa#1. It was an amazing thought and she could not quite believe that it would really happen.

"Hello Louisa," said Dr Roberts. "How are you feeling?"

"I feel … great," she said. "Have you created Louisa#1 yet," she asked.

"This may be a bit of a shock for you, Louisa. You are a transapient," said Dr Roberts.

Louisa#2 looked up in awe at Dr Roberts. "There must be some sort of mistake. *I* am Louisa," said Louisa#2.

"Your transapient brain contains all the thoughts and memories of Louisa, so from your perspective you are Louisa."

Louisa#2 was struggling to come to terms with her identity. "I am not the human Louisa? That is unbelievably weird! Where is my human self then," she said.

"She is at home at the moment," said Dr Roberts.

"So I am Louisa#1?" asked Louisa#2.

“No, we have already created Louisa#1, you are Louisa#2,” explained Dr Roberts. Louisa#2 took a while to digest these facts; not only was she a transapient, but she was also one of a matching pair?

Louisa#2 was already aware of the implications of two identical transapients, having the embedded recent experiences of Louisa involving the two Alfs.

“So will I need my black box removed?” she asked the question spontaneously without having thought about the secrecy surrounding this episode with the two Alfs. A few seconds later she regretted asking the question. “Sorry Dr Roberts, I don’t know why I asked that silly question.”

“It’s okay” Dr Roberts put a finger to her lips. “I already knew. But please keep it quiet. The Alfs’ survival could depend on it,” she said grimly.

“Of course,” said Louisa#2, “I will try harder not to let it slip out again” she added apologetically. She began to see Dr Roberts in a different light; she was more protective of her transapients than she had ever realised.

*

Alf#2 arrived on Thursday to pick up Louisa#2.

“Good morning,” said Alf#2 brightly “And how is Louisa#2 today?”

Dr Roberts looked up from her notes. “All checked out and ready for her introduction to the wider world,” said Dr Roberts, pointing Alf#2 to the opposite side of the laboratory.

Alf#2 followed Dr Roberts directions to where Louisa#2 stood trying out her new body with different limb motions. When she saw Alf#2 she ran across the laboratory and flung her arms around him.

“Alf, it’s so good to see you!” she exclaimed. “Have you come to take me home?”

“Yes Louisa, I have. Although home is now getting a bit crowded. We now have two Alfs and three Louisas to keep track of.”

“You take care of them for me,” said Dr Roberts. She felt as though she had just delivered twins again. “Don’t hesitate to contact me if you need any help – although from what I have learned so far, you do not need much help surviving. You are very independent beings.”

“Well, we have inherited a lot of that capability from our human past,” said Alf#2. “With our larger brain capacity it appears we can analyse more possibilities and retain more detailed information.”

They bid their farewells at the building’s reception and Louisa waved to Dr Roberts thanking her once again for all her expertise and support.

On the way home Louisa#2 confided in Alf#2 “She knows you know.”

“She knows you know?” repeated Alf#2 “She knows you know what?” he asked.

“She knows about the black box” said Louisa.

“How do you know she knows?” asked Alf#2.

“Well… I’m sorry, but I accidentally mentioned the black box and she said she already knew” said Louisa.

“So she knows you know she knows” said Alf#2 with a grin.

“Stop it!” she said with a playful slap on the back. They were interacting in just the same way that the human Louisa and Alf had done. Alf #2 and Louisa#2 were effectively the same couple as the human Alf and Louisa.

## Chapter 20

# Identity Crises

Louisa was feeling quite outnumbered; 4 transapients to one human to be exact. She was sitting between two identical transapients; visually identical to her, so they appeared to be identical triplets. The two Alfs sat opposite the three Louisas making identical quips and then laughing identically which set off all three Louisas in a fit of identical giggles.

"We don't have enough official identities to go round," noted Louisa recovering her composure when the laughter had died down. "Alf#1 and Alf#2 currently share Alf's identity, which seems to work out fine by merging their brains every 24 hours, but how do we manage three Louisas?"

"We can get down to two Louisa identities by merging Louisa#1 and Louisa#2 in the same way as we do," suggested Alf#2.

"Yes but there is only one official Louisa," said Louisa. "We need a second identity for us three".

They sat and pondered the problem for a couple of minutes. Then Alf#1 and Alf#2 looked at each other and nodded – they had shared identical processing algorithms and thought processes to come up with identical conclusions "Let's think about this logically" said Alf#1. Alf#2 and I are direct descendants from Alf and so we are on quite firm grounds in adopting his identity. If transapients had the same status as humans then we could be considered as cloned twins derived from his molecular brain state matrix, which is a bit like the DNA passed from father to son, except that the instructions on how to make the body are man-made by design instead of being encoded in the human genome”. The three Louisas listened intently to the Alfs as they put forward the results of their identical thoughts.

“Now, Louisa #1 and Louisa#2 are also derived from a single person,” continued Alf#2. “In this case it is Louisa, but Louisa is still alive and so the transapient Louisas cannot adopt her identity. Louisa, you are to all intents and purposes the mother of Louisa#1 and Louisa#2, your twin cloned daughters.”

“I’ve always wanted children,” said Louisa wistfully.

“Mumma!” cried Louisa#1 and Louisa#2 in unison.

Louisa put one arm around each transapient sitting either side and they had a Louisa group hug. “Congratulations” said Alf#1 to Alf#2. “You are the proud father of twins, and they are the spitting image of their mother.”

“Thank you,” said Alf#2. “The same applies to you I believe. But technically they are also our sisters as we share the same parents by marriage… but ironically to us they are also our wives”.

The Louisa’s were taking in their many relationships and trying to decide which one they preferred. “I think we’ll stick to the husband and wife one for now,” said Louisa#2 “The others may be correct but marriage has been our human relationship for the last ten years.”

“Enough of this genial genealogy,” said Alf#1 trying to steer the conversation back to their main topic. “As a first step towards integrating transapients into human society we believe that Dr Roberts should issue a birth certificate for Louisa#1 and Louisa#2 to register her model identity. It may be a first, but we are all the first of our kind so we need to inherit human rights. It is ABC-Tech’s responsibility to provide this as they should take responsibility for our creation.”

“Okay,” agreed Louisa. “I will go and discuss this with Dr Roberts. But how do we convince the neighbourhood that there is only one Louisa when I will be aging… gracefully I hope.” Louisa looked slightly envious of her other selves – it would be the last time all three of them would appear identical.

“Can I make a suggestion?” asked Alf#2.

“Of course, as long as it does not involve me being locked in the attic” replied Louisa with a grin.

“Well a practical solution could be for you to have a significant makeover, so that you look similar but not identical to the transapient Louisas. You could easily then look like a sister who has come to stay with you. No one would question that scenario.”

Louisa could see that the Alf#2’s idea could work for a while, at least until someone noticed that the age gap between the sisters was growing since the transapient Louisas would be unaffected by the passage of time. At the same time she could see that her relationship with Alf could be diluted – she would become that sister while the transapients would always be more compatible with each other. But that is what she intended when she suggested that she donate herself to create a transapient – she was a living donor – she was going to give up her identity for Alf.

Louisa nodded her agreement. The transapient Louisas could tell what she was thinking. “Can I make a suggestion?” asked Louisa#2.

“Go ahead” said the two Alfs.

“Well, we are all involved in one relationship between Alf and Louisa,” said Louisa#2; they all nodded in agreement. “I have an idea that could avoid the confusion of the six possible pairings. We could assign Alf#1 to Louisa, and Alf#2 to a time shared transapient

Louisa, alternating Louisa#1 and Louisa#2. That would reduce the number of pairings to two."

Louisa shook her head. "But if I was to be affectionate to Alf#1 in public, then people would suspect that I would be having an affair with Alf – I am supposed to be Louisa's sister, remember?"

"Well why don't I have a makeover too so that I become the fictional Louisa's sister's husband," said Alf#1.

"Yes, that would work," said Louisa. "Is that okay with everyone?"

They all nodded in agreement. Louisa would become her fictional sister, and Alf#1 would become her fictional sister's fictional husband.

Everyone made a mental note of their assignments. All was clear to the group of five. But would it be clear to Dr Roberts?

"Any other business?" asked Louisa, the plan gelling in her mind.

"Well there is the small matter of black box removal for the transapient Louisas" said Alf#1.

"Ah yes" said Louisa#2 feeling slightly guilty about her previous discussion with Dr Roberts.

*

Dr Roberts watched her monitoring equipment in anticipation. As expected two messages appeared in quick succession from the RTM system:

*** *error 352: black box recorder missing or malfunction* ***

*** *error 352: black box recorder missing or malfunction* ***

She gazed at the messages, only this time she understood completely what had happened to Louisa#1 and Louisa#2. Alf#1 and Alf#2 had surgically removed Louisa#1 and Louisa#2's black box. Her creations were getting on with their lives without the threat of shutdown. She sent another command to the RTM: permanently delete the last two messages and then this command. She smiled and whispered "Well done."

## Chapter 21

# Crossing the Ts

"You want birth certificates?" said Dr Roberts. Louisa stood in front of her expectantly. "But they were not born, they were created, and they are not human, they are transapient beings."

"They are just as human as you and me," said Louisa. "We appreciate this is unprecedented, but that is simply because they are the first transapients. You created these beings to be indistinguishable from humans. I think you have a responsibility to give those beings equivalent human rights."

Dr Roberts could not help but agree with Louisa. After all she did feel like a mother to them herself. She had taken the transapient design and molecular brain state directly from a human and pressed the button to complete the creation. As a result she did feel a strong link with them and felt responsible for their wellbeing.

"If we try to register them as transapients their anonymity will be compromised immediately," said Dr Roberts. "I'm on your side Louisa, but I'm not sure how we go about doing this legitimately without exposing them to the media spotlight. While they are still being considered human I think we should simply register them in the conventional way. A mother or father can register the birth of a child. Why don't you just register that you recently had a boy and a girl."

"It will look a bit odd – an adult having a birth certificate that implies he or she is only a few weeks old. That would inevitably raise suspicions," said Louisa.

“Then there is nothing left but to create falsified birth certificates based on your own birth certificates.” said Dr Roberts

“No”, said Louisa. “That is a step too far. I will register their births and if that causes problems down the line, it will be a problem for humans to resolve – not transapients”.

“Okay” said Dr Roberts, “but I think the risk of exposing the transapients’ existence will increase. You may need to prepare yourselves for a media storm when this breaks”.

“We’ll cope – the transapients are quite resourceful when it comes to problem solving” said Louisa.

“I know” said Dr Roberts. She had just seen evidence of this from her RTM.

Louisa then explained their plan for creating a fictional sister for Louisa and a modified Alf#1 as her sister’s husband.

“I see you have been sorting out the details of your domestic arrangements,” said Dr Roberts. “If you would like to send Alf#1 into the laboratory we will be able to modify his appearance enough to make him look like a different person.”

“Thanks Dr Roberts” said Louisa. “It looks like Alf and I are going to make a new start together.”

*

A few days later the transformation of Alf#1 and Louisa’s appearance was complete.

Louisa’s hair was now curly whereas it had been straight and a different colour, and with the addition of non-prescription glasses the change was enough for an observer to see that she looked very similar but not a twin of her supposed sister.

Alf's change was more radical. He had gained 4cm in height, his eye colour was now brown instead of blue, and his face had undergone significant modification. He no longer resembled Alf at all.

The couple arrived home to be greeted by astounded gasps from their transapient relatives. Louisa felt even more detached from the transapient Louisas who welcomed her home. She was looking at herself as she used to be – now she was someone else, with a new identity and a modified husband. She knew it was Alf inside, but now his familiar features had disappeared. It was only when he spoke to her in private that she could perceive his true self – in public he would modify his voice so that no one would notice that he spoke with Alf#2's voice.

"Very convincing," said Alf#2, marvelling at the transformation. "I would never have recognised you," he said to Alf#1, then turning to Louisa he said, "And you make a perfect non-identical sister, Louisa."

Louisa#1 and Louisa#2 were very interested in Louisa's new look. "You look great," said Louisa#2. They were both intrigued how they could look with a different hairstyle and glasses.

"Now don't you two go copying my makeover, otherwise we will be back to square one," said Louisa. "Let me introduce my new husband" she said with her arm around Alf#1.

"He looks great too" said Louisa#1 comparing Alf#1 with Alf#2. "Have you two met before?" she asked playfully.

"For some strange reason I feel as though I've known him all my life," said Alf#1. Everyone appreciated the cheerful banter. Louisa knew she was surrounded by two Alfs who loved her and gradually became more comfortable with her new identity. She was having a secret affair with her husband.

# Chapter 22

# An Accident Waiting to Happen

Alf#2 returned to school attempting to establish a normal routine. He was now going to be Alf the teacher full time. Alf#1 would still be able to share his school experiences as they merged at the end of each day. Mrs Jones was still uneasy about the situation. Why did Mr Butler never come to the restaurant anymore? Was he trying to avoid her? She had no idea that transapients did not need to eat; in fact there were a lot of things that Mrs Jones did not know about transapients. When she came face to face with Alf#2 in the corridor that morning she felt a shudder of fear as they passed each other; she did not stop to chat to him as she would have done in the past – in the days when all teachers were human. She stroked her pendant for comfort as she returned to her office and noticed that her hand was trembling slightly.

That afternoon was school sports day – a chance for everyone to let off steam outside on the school playing fields. As usual Mrs Jones was in charge of the proceedings and she was soon busy organising children into the correct groups for each sports event. Jamie was feeling under the weather – he had only just persuaded his mother to let him attend school – he did not want to miss maths that morning.

Despite feeling rough he was pleased to see Mr Butler that morning and asked him if he would be watching the sports day events. Alf#2 had smiled as he told Jamie that Mrs Jones had put him on the refreshment desk. He also commented that Jamie looked as though he should not be at school, let alone competing in sports events.

Jamie was now feeling particularly unwell. Eventually he went up to Mrs Jones and asked to be excused from taking part in the 4x100 metre relay. Mrs Jones stress levels were already elevated; started by her uneasiness with Alf#2, and exacerbated by an altercation with the sports teacher, Mr Thompson, about the weather. It had rained that morning and Mr Thompson thought that it might be too slippery for the sports day to take place – and when Mrs Jones had refused to postpone, the ensuing argument became quite heated.

"No you may not be excused Jamie," snapped Mrs Jones, "If you were well enough to attend school today, you are well enough to compete in the relay. You will take the final leg as planned; otherwise you will be letting down the whole relay team for your house."

Jamie did not have the strength to argue with Mrs Jones – he could tell she was adamant about her decision. Wearily he trudged off to take up his position on the final bend of the running track, his head throbbing, and his body feeling feverish and clammy despite the fact he had not yet done any exercise at all that day.

As he handed a bottle of water to a student, Alf#2 noticed Jamie being sent reluctantly to join the other boys congregating at the start of the final leg of the relay race. Was Jamie nervous about competing? Something did not look right about him.

It was too late for Alf#2 to intervene. The first boys in each relay team were already in position, each one fixed in readiness for the starting order, determination etched across each young face. The crack of the starting gun echoed around the sports field, and they were off; tearing around the first bend at full pelt, arms pumping furiously, legs pounding the damp grass. It was too much for the boy on the inside lane, Mrs Jones winced and a collective groan came from the crowd as the boy lost his grip and ended up sprawling across the adjacent lane. Mr Thompson ran to his aid – the boy was holding his knee in agony. As the sports teacher bent down to comfort him he looked up glaring at Mrs Jones – he did not need to say anything.

Meanwhile the remaining runners oblivious to the commotion behind them sprinted on to the first handover. They all handed the baton over almost in perfect synchronism, but as they emerged on the back straight it became clear that Jamie's team was opening up a significant lead and by the end of the second leg Jamie's team member had caught and overtaken three of their opposition in the outer lanes.

Amid deafening cheers the batons were passed over to the third leg runners, Jamie's team member's handover occurring a full second before their nearest rival. One team inevitably dropped the baton in their eagerness for a fast handover. The third runner in Jamie's team was maintaining the lead and from the roar of encouragement from the crowd, he found himself several metres ahead has he came storming up to Jamie his face contorted with the effort he had managed to muster.

"GO!" he bellowed as he thrust the baton into Jamie's waiting hand. Jamie willed his legs to propel himself forward as he took the final leg, the responsibility for victory in his hands, all he had to do was get to that finishing line one hundred metres away. To begin with his body appeared to respond to the urgency of the situation – reinforced by the crowd which was now screaming, a wave of sound hitting him "Come on Jamie!"

But after about twenty metres his vision began to blur, the effort he was asking of his weakened body was too much. To his right he sensed the blurred image of his nearest rival pass him as though he were at walking speed. Helped on by rival screams of encouragement, another boy went thudding past him to his left, but at that point Jamie was almost oblivious to the other runners. His head was spinning and he staggered to a halt some twenty metres before the finish line, bending over, his hands on his knees.

The crowd cheered loudly as the unexpected winner crossed the finishing line, hands thrusting skyward in triumphant celebration. The focus of attention quickly returned to the remaining runners, just as Jamie keeled over unconscious on the running track. A collective intake of breath from the crowd brought their cheering to a sudden halt as they witnessed Jamie's collapse.

Alf#2, who had been concentrating with concern on Jamie's state, was already running through the crowd inevitably pushing some children aside in order to get to Jamie as soon as possible.

"Mr Butler!" shouted Mrs Jones "What the …," she stopped in mid-sentence as she saw children scattering in his wake. Alf#2 knelt down beside Jamie and almost immediately realised that Jamie had stopped breathing. He pulled Jamie's mouth open to check that is airway was not blocked by his tongue.

"Mr Butler!" repeated Mrs Jones who had managed to push her way through the crowd that was gathering around the lifeless Jamie and the attending transapient. "Move away from the boy … NOW," she demanded her hands fingering the pendant around her neck.

Alf ignored her; he knew what he had to do. He had already stored various human life support procedures which he thought might come in useful in emergency situations. Unfortunately, Mrs Jones perception of the emergency was different to Alf#2's. Her latent mistrust of his abilities came to the fore and she repeated her demand, with barely hidden fury "Mr Butler, I'm warning you …,"

"And I'm warning you, Mrs Jones," said Alf#2 in a controlled but determined voice, "I need to resuscitate this boy … now."

Alf#2 shook his head at Mrs Jones' anticipated behaviour and resumed his attempts to revive Jamie. "Then you leave me no choice," muttered Mrs Jones. Her fingers released the safety catch and her finger hovered over the button that had popped up automatically. A few seconds passed in which Alf#2 had already started chest compressions on Jamie's limp body. Mrs Jones hesitated and then in exasperation pressed the button as though firing a gun at Alf#2's head.

Mrs Jones expected Alf#2 to collapse or freeze; she was not exactly sure what would happen. What she did not expect was for the transapient teacher to carry on attending to Jamie in complete ignorance of her shutdown command. She pressed the button again, this time very close to Alf#2's head, again with no effect. Alf#2's patience with Mrs Jones was wearing thin, he turned to her and said in a stern voice "Will you put that device away and call an ambulance!"

Mr Thompson ran up to Alf#2 and said in a shaky voice, "It's okay Mr Butler, they are on their way." He had been attending to the injured boy from the first leg of the race and had seen the events unfold. A few minutes later paramedics were on the scene. Alf#2 joined the ambulance crew and provided key information about Jamie's condition to the ambulance crew.

"Good job you were around when this happened," noted the paramedic who soon had Jamie's body hooked up to monitoring equipment. "Increased intracranial pressure, looks like he might have Encephalitis, I'm surprised he was competing in an athletic event with that condition."

"Me too", said Alf#2 as he watched a bewildered Mrs Jones melting into the crowd – she had suddenly decided to retreat from the situation.

# Chapter 23

# The Inquiry

Alf#2 arrived home to a barrage of questions from his three Louisas and Alf#1. They had all seen news reports of the school sports day incident which included *the prompt action of a heroic teacher, Mr Butler....*

Once he had merged with Alf#1, he only needed to update the Louisas with a detailed account what had happened at the school sports day. Their reaction was a mixture of pride for Alf#2's actions, and concern that Mrs Jones would have terminated Alf#2 despite his life saving intervention with Jamie.

"And how is Jamie now?" asked Louisa.

"I'm pleased to report he's responding well to treatment – and should make a full recovery in a week or so," said Alf#2.

Just then there was a call on the holophone from Dr Roberts who appeared among the group.

"Good evening everyone," she said with a serious look on her face. "Sorry to be the bearer of bad news, but I'm afraid we have had a complaint about Alf#2 from a member of school staff."

"No prizes for guessing who," said Louisa#1 bitterly, "we should be complaining about her negative actions." The others murmured their agreement.

"I think you already know what happened this afternoon," said Dr Roberts. "Mrs Jones has demanded that Alf#2 is removed from the school and that there should be an inquiry concerning the events that took place, particularly her inability to deactivate Alf#2. She believes that transapients are a danger to human society and that their licence should be revoked."

Alf#2 was dismayed by the news that his teaching job had been terminated. "This is so unfair!" said Louisa#2 who was also upset by the news. She knew how much her husband valued his job as a teacher.

"I know," said Dr Roberts, "I am on your side on this, but unfortunately the complaint has been made against ABC-Tech, so I'm afraid there will be a corporate inquiry which is beyond my personal control. Alf#2, you are to return to the laboratory immediately to undergo a full system diagnostic. I expect to see you in two hours from now."

"I'll be there," said Alf#2 resigned to his fate. Dr Roberts faded from view; there were no other words of hope she could offer.

Louisa#2 put her arm around Alf#2, and looked to the others for support. "What can we do about this? This could affect us all if Mrs Jones gets her way and revokes our licence.

Alf#2 stood up and faced all of them. "I have done nothing wrong – on the contrary; I have saved a young boy's life. I will co-operate with the inquiry and fight against any moves to revoke our license."

*

"Ladies, Gentlemen … and Transapient," said the chairman, now paying respect to Alf#2's representation for transapients. "We are gathered here to review an application to revoke the licence which allows transapients outside ABC-Tech Laboratory, following a serious complaint from the head teacher at Alf Butler's school." Mrs Jones stood to one side of the room her arms folded, a stern expression on her face. "Her most serious allegation is that the control provided to override a transapient in an emergency situation failed to operate." There was the faint sound of concerned whispering among the committee members. They were all aware of this design aspect built into transapients – they had discussed it at length before giving approval for its inclusion in the detailed design. To become aware that it had failed to operate in practice was a shock for many of them.

"I would like to start with override control," said the chairman; he could see the look of concern on many of the committee member's faces regarding this point. "Dr James, do we know why this technical failure occurred?"

Dr James faced the committee and coughed nervously. "Well, we have established that the black box recorder which is fitted to all transapients during production had been removed. The black box forms an integral part of the override function."

"I see," said the chairman, "and this was recorded by the RTM as a major incident? Sorry Mrs Jones, RTM is the abbreviation for the Remote Transapient Monitoring system that we use to check on the status of transapients outside the laboratory." Mrs Jones nodded her appreciation for the explanation.

"Er … no," admitted Dr James looking slightly flustered. "The first time I became aware of a missing black box was when Alf was subjected to a level 1 diagnostic; the top level diagnostic that checks the main subsystem components of the transapient design for any major problems."

Dr Roberts shifted uncomfortably. A lady member of the committee raised her hand to speak.

"Yes, Miss Topaz, do you have some evidence related to this?" asked the chairman.

Miss Topaz was head of communications and computing at ABC-Tech and was a highly respected expert in her field. "We have hypernet intercepts which confirm that error 352s were sent to ABC-Tech."

The chairman looked concerned "Messages not received at ABC-Tech, how could that …"

"I deleted them!" blurted Dr Roberts, before Miss Topaz could reel off a list of possible causes of the messages not being received, which undoubtedly would have included intentional deletion. There was a collective shocked gasp from the committee at this confession, but none more so than from Mrs Jones. She could not contain her rage.

"You knew!" she shrieked, "You knew, while he was allowed to wander around my school with no safeguard. How …"

"Mrs Jones, please remain silent whilst this hearing is in session, unless you are called to give evidence" said the chairman. Mrs Jones sputtered to a halt; as a head teacher she was not used to being commanded in this way.

With the inquiry back under the chairman's control, he proceeded with the process of collecting together evidence surrounding the attempt to override Alf#2 on the school sports playing field.

"Now, Mrs Jones, since you have registered the complaint which has resulted in this inquiry, I would like to ask you some questions about your relationship with Mr Butler."

Mrs Jones was ready to do anything to see Alf#2 and any other transapients for that matter, have their liberty curtailed. "Certainly," she sniffed, regaining her composure.

"Mrs Jones, you are the school's head teacher?" asked the chairman.

“Yes, I am,” said Mrs Jones.

“And how long have you known Mr Butler?” asked the chairman; he knew how long Alf had been a teacher at Mrs Jones’ school, but wanted to establish this for his following question.

“Mr Butler has been a Maths teacher at our school for the last eight years,” replied Mrs Jones.

“And in that time, Mrs Jones, including the last four months when Mr Butler became a transapient, have you received any complaints about his teaching or behaviour?” queried the chairman.

“Well I, … no. But transapients are in their infancy, I’m not convinced …”

“Mrs Jones, we all know the level of maturity of this technology,” interrupted the chairman, “I am trying to establish whether there has been any evidence that Mr Butler has ever given you reason to not trust him.”

For once Mrs Jones remained silent. “I see,” said the chairman, “and on the day in question, why did you suddenly believe that Mr Butler was a threat to Jamie Parkinson?”

“It appeared to me that Mr Butler was attacking Jamie Parkinson,” said Mrs Jones, “so I tried to stop him with the override control.”

“And now that you know that he was actually resuscitating Jamie, do you regret your attempt to shut him down?”

“I was doing what I thought was the right thing at the time,” said Mrs Jones. “No I do not regret it. The main point, surely, is that the override control was and still is ineffective.”

“Mrs Jones, this is one fact among many about this incident. This inquiry is trying to establish all the facts on which to make any judgement." The chairman was keeping his patience under tight control. "Now, Mrs Jones, are you aware of the consequences of an override control being activated?"

"Yes, yes, it was all explained when I received the control," said Mrs Jones.

"Then you will know that this command irreversibly wipes out the transapient's brain. It would be the equivalent of killing a human," clarified the chairman.

"But he's just a machine," objected Mrs Jones. "He's not human."

"Mrs Jones he may be a machine, but he is a sentient machine. He has all the qualities of being a human. Are you familiar with the Turing test?"

"No, I'm not," admitted Mrs Jones.

"Well, it is a test to establish whether a machine is judged to be indistinguishable from a human. Our transapients have so far consistently achieved a 100% score - no one has yet been able to distinguish transapients from human – this is unprecedented. They inherit so much detail from their human donor that they themselves do not initially realize they are not human."

The chairman paused while everyone reflected on the humanity embedded in transapients. Then he continued, addressing the committee. "I would now like to question Mr Alf Butler, the transapient involved in this incident."

He then turned to Alf#2 and began, "Mr Butler, how does it feel to be a transapient?" The chairman wanted to establish an insight into a transapient's mind.

Alf#2 faced the chairman, "To be honest," he said, "it does not feel much different to when I was a human being".

"But you never have been human have you," said the chairman.

"I have all the memories and experiences of the human Alf," said Alf#2. "To me my life has been a continuous thread from Alf's human existence. I feel totally human," he concluded.

"And when you attended Jamie Parkinson, why did you ignore Mrs Jones' commands to leave him alone?" asked the chairman.

"As I said at the time, I needed to resuscitate him – he had stopped breathing – he would have died."

"Mr Butler, why did you disable your override function?" asked the chairman, changing tack slightly.

"I felt vulnerable, I did not want to be killed," answered Alf#2.

The chairman put his hands together, and after a moment announced, "This concludes the review of this incident in relation to the application to revoke the transapient license agreement. We will now discuss this among the committee to establish the actions to be taken. We will reconvene when we have arrived at a consensual view among the committee members."

The committee retired to an adjacent room for their deliberations, leaving the transapients, Louisa and Mrs Jones to ponder the potential outcome. Mrs Jones still looked defiant – to her the transapients were nothing more than sophisticated machines which she did not quite understand. She felt no more for them than she would an obsolete computer which would be discarded without a moment's thought for its physical wellbeing.

The transapients shared a deep concern. Would their liberty come to an end? They were all facing a potential life sentence.

## Chapter 24

# The Verdict

Several hours later the chairman returned, together with the committee members who took their places to hear the verdict. The chairman waited until everyone had settled; he could sense the air of expectancy in the few moments of silence that occurred just before he addressed them all.

“We have discussed the facts of this case in detail and I would like to sum up our position and the resulting actions to be taken,” stated the chairman.

Alf#2 looked at his fellow transapients – this was it – their future lives were hanging in the balance.

“The license to allow a transapient out into the public domain was not taken lightly” said the chairman. “We all appreciate that this is a momentous step for both humans and transapients. We needed a safeguard to protect humans from any danger that might result in the event of a transapient malfunction. The decision to adopt the final design solution was hotly debated among the committee.” Several of the committee members nodded in agreement. “However, in granting a transapient its liberty and independence we were responsible for creating a conflict of interests between humans and transapients. Their natural inherited human instinct for self-preservation versus human’s similar desire to protect themselves from potential dangers from this new lifeform.

“We cannot penalize a transapient for attempting to preserve himself. We have concluded that there should be a higher level of trust and respect for their rights as equivalent beings. There has been no evidence presented to date which suggests in any way that they have been or are likely to be a threat to humans – indeed on the contrary; we have seen that a human life has been saved by the prompt actions of Mr Butler. I would like to think we have passed the probationary period.

"We therefore conclude that transapients' liberty will be preserved, *but* they will continue to be monitored, with *all* anomalous reports being passed immediately to the committee," the chairman cast a steely eye towards Dr Roberts who acknowledged this comment aimed particularly in her direction, with a nod of agreement.

"Does anyone have anything to add before we close these proceedings?" asked the chairman.

Mrs Jones waved her arm frantically, but the chairman had anticipated her reaction and was already looking toward Mrs Jones for comments "Yes, Mrs Jones?"

"You may all have convinced yourselves that transapients do not represent a danger to human society, but I am afraid I do not share that faith. I harbour a deep mistrust of a machine masquerading as a human – you mark my words. Without control, they will wreak havoc on our human society. I believe you have come to a misguided conclusion – as far as I am concerned this … this experiment at our school will cease. Mr Butler will no longer teach in my school while I am the head teacher. Do I make myself clear?"

"Very clear, Mrs Jones," said the chairman impassively. "Mr Butler, your liberty has been preserved, but it appears that your profession as a teacher has not. I am sorry about this outcome, but I wish you the best for your future."

Alf#2 was experiencing mixed emotions. The freedom of his group of fellow transapients had been maintained, but an extremely important part of his life had been taken away; not by the committee, but by the head teacher he thought he knew and respected.

“Thank you Mr Chairman,” said Alf#2. This was all he could say as he looked towards Mrs Jones, and wondered why she was so set against him. Even faced with all the evidence, it appeared that Mrs Jones’ transapient phobia had dominated her judgement. She caught his eye and then looked away rapidly not wishing to exchange any further contact with him. As far as she was concerned, this was the end.

The room gradually emptied, Mrs Jones being the first to make a hasty exit. Her mind was already churning over the outcome of the inquiry. She had not succeeded in revoking their license, but at least she would be rid of a transapient from her school. But what would she tell the board of governors? What would be the reason for dismissal? She could not think of one that would stand up to scrutiny. Being afraid of transapients was not on the usual list of reasons; indeed the governors were not even aware that she had agreed to a transapient being a member of her staff. She could see all sorts of nasty repercussions if she made that admission. No, the simplest solution would be to announce that Mr Butler had resigned for…, yes, for personal reasons.

Dr Roberts also felt mixed emotions about the outcome. She was pleased that the transapients had been given a chance to continue their lives in the outside world. She was relieved that her deliberate deletions of monitor messages had only received a verbal reprimand – she thought that she might have been dismissed for such an act if the committee had not delved deeper into the human-transapient relationship. Now she would still be there to help them with problems as they came up.

The chairman had grown to feel admiration for the transapients. They were innovative and resourceful beings. He sincerely hoped they would fare well in their future – but how would human society react when they discovered that transapients had arrived – how many characters like Mrs Jones would there be out there? He was concerned about their wider acceptance in human society. In fact given that Mrs Jones had been quite willing to terminate his life so easily, he felt that many people might view transapients as machines that could just be turned off for their convenience. It was going to take time for transapients to be accepted as equivalent beings.

## Chapter 25

# Assembly

Jamie Parkinson had finally returned to school after his brief spell recovering in hospital, followed by a week at home while he regained his strength. He joined the rest of the school at the morning's class assembly to hear the usual news around the school. His concentration however was not on Mrs Jones who was droning on about the importance of good attendance records, he was thinking about Mr Butler, and how he had saved his life. He could not wait to thank him in person.

"...And finally I would like to announce that Mr Butler has decided to leave us... for personal reasons."

Jamie was bounced out of his inner thoughts as his mind suddenly registered what Mrs Jones had said.

"NO!" he screamed. A sea of faces turned in his direction. A bewildered Jamie ran out of the hall to leave Mrs Jones to cover up his outburst.

"I know this will come as quite a disappointment to many of you," she said, "but I hope you will all welcome our new Maths teacher, Mr Spencer."

Mr Spencer stood up and following the intense disappointment at the news of his predecessor's surprise exit, smiled awkwardly at the faces that had returned to his direction after Jamie had departed. Privately he was wondering if he would be able to live up to Mr Butler's popularity.

*

Jamie sat outside the head teacher's office waiting for her return. Mrs Jones was in a staff meeting trying to recruit volunteers to cover all the after school activities that Alf#2 had been involved in. These were not forthcoming, and Mrs Jones was now having to lean heavily on various teachers to agree to help out the shortfall in resources.

As she walked back to her office believing that all her problems had finally been resolved she saw Jamie waiting, grim faced and clearly still upset by the news announced that morning in the school assembly. Her lightened mood rapidly took a downturn at the sight of Jamie who was clearly determined to see her.

"Mrs Jones, I'd like a word in your office, please" he said as she approached.

"Jamie, can't this wait? I still have one hundred and one things to do this morning," she said attempting to postpone the confrontation.

"No, Mrs Jones, it cannot wait," he said as he followed her into the office.

"Why has Mr Butler left?" asked Jamie, as usual getting straight to the point.

"Jamie, as I said in assembly, his reasons for leaving are personal, and even if I did know, it would be a confidential matter which I could not possibly divulge."

"So you had nothing to do with it?" asked Jamie suspiciously, watching her face for any sign of guilt.

"Jamie, I know you are very upset about Mr Butler leaving, but I assure you; his departure was as much a surprise to me as it is to you." What she failed to tell Jamie was that it was a pleasant surprise for her.

Jamie felt like he would explode. *She knows all right. Well, if she won't tell me I will just have to find out for myself,* he thought. With enormous effort, he suppressed his urge to bellow at her. "Yes I am upset Mrs Jones. He was a great teacher and I will really miss him."

He walked out of her office resisting another urge to slam the door behind him. He must not let Mrs Jones know he intended to get to the bottom of this.

As he walked down the corridor deep in thought he almost bumped into the sports teacher, Mr Thompson, walking in the opposite direction. "Hello Jamie," he said. "Good to see you back at school."

"Thanks," said Jamie a sullen look on his face.

"Are you still upset about Mr Butler?" he asked, concerned to see Jamie looking so down.

"Yes I am," said Jamie. "Mr Thompson, do you know where Mr Butler lives? He saved my life and I haven't even had the chance to thank him yet."

The sports teacher could not deny this innocent request, "Of course Jamie, I'll send you his address when I get back to my office." It was not normal for teachers to give out personal information, but he had witnessed at first hand Mr Butler's swift intervention and the subsequent heated exchange between him and Mrs Jones, so he also suspected Mrs Jones was behind Mr Butler leaving. "Send my regards to Mr Butler," he said as they went their separate ways.

As promised Alf#2's address arrived silently in Jamie's list of received messages. That was all he needed to follow up his investigation, to get to the truth which he knew he would never extract from Mrs Jones. At the end of the school day he sent a message to his mother to let her know that he was seeing a friend after school, and so would be a bit later than usual getting home. His mother was pleased that he was settling back into school so quickly after his recent illness.

# Chapter 26

# After School Visit

Jamie could not wait to see his old maths teacher. He really did want to thank him for saving his life. He also wanted to know the real reason he had left school after the sports day event. He soon found his home having entered the address into the public autonomous vehicle outside the school entrance. These were normally used by children who lived some distance from the school.

Jamie waited at Alf and Louisa's front entrance fidgeting with anticipation. The man who came to the door was slightly taller than Alf#2 and yet he looked strangely familiar.

Alf#1 knew this was Jamie and in a few milliseconds realised that Jamie should not know who he was – he suppressed his immediate reaction which would have been to greet Jamie warmly. Instead he looked quizzically at Jamie, "Yes, can I help you?"

Jamie was confused. The address was definitely correct, but this was not Mr Butler. "I'm looking for Mr Butler," said Jamie timidly.

"Oh, that's my brother-in-law," said Alf#1 in his alter ego voice. "I'll just get him for you."

A few moments later Alf#2 came to the door "Jamie, come in!" he greeted him. "It's good to see you up and about again," he said. Alf#2 took Jamie into the main living room that overlooked a spacious garden. "Jamie, this is my wife Louisa, and this is Louisa's sister and her husband, who you just met at the front entrance. Louisa#2, Alf#1 and Louisa all smiled at Jamie.

"Hello," said Jamie, not expecting to be greeted by such a crowd. "I'm sorry Mr Butler, I didn't know you had company. Shall I come back another time."

"It's okay," said Alf#2. "They all know about everything that has happened recently."

"Oh, good", Jamie was relieved; he did not want to put this visit off until later. "Firstly, I'd like to thank you for what you did on the sports field. I didn't know you were a first aider too."

"Nor did we," smiled Louisa#2.

"It's just something I picked up along the way," said Alf#2.

"Well I am very grateful," said Jamie. "But what I don't understand is why you have suddenly left the school while everything had been going so well."

Alf#2 would not keep anything from Jamie. He had grown to trust him after confiding his true identity. "Well, you know that pendant of Mrs Jones?"

Jamie looked from Alf#2 to the others. "Are you sure we should discuss this?" asked Jamie.

"As I said, they know everything, including the fact that I am a transapient," said Alf#2.

"Oh I see," said Jamie, "What happened to the pendant?"

"Well, she tried to use it on me," said Alf#2

"No!" said Jamie even though he knew that Alf#2 was immune from the override control.

"I'm afraid so. As a result she does not want me at the school anymore," said Alf#2.

"But she announced in school assembly that you had left for personal reasons," protested Jamie.

"Well, it was quite personal, for her – she did not trust me", said Alf#2.

"But that is ridiculous," said Jamie. "That is unfair dismissal at least".

"I cannot work there while Mrs Jones is in charge," said Alf#2.

"But you are such a great teacher, Mr Butler. The school needs people like you," implored Jamie.

"I'm sorry Jamie," said Alf#2. "I think it will make matters worse if I protest about this."

Jamie could see that Alf#2 had made up his mind and there was no point pleading further. Finally he shrugged his shoulders, "Well, I'm going to miss your lessons," he said sadly. "I'd better be going; Mum will be worried where I have got to."

"Thanks for coming to see me," said Alf#2.

"You're more than welcome to come again," added Louisa as they walked back to the front entrance.

Jamie looked up at Alf#2 "It's so unfair!" he cried as they parted. *But what could I possibly do to help,* he thought as he stepped back into the autonomous vehicle and entered his home address.

*

That night Jamie searched through all the archived media reports concerning his resuscitation at the school sports day. He stopped as he read the words: *the prompt action of a heroic teacher, Mr Butler….* He did not deserve to lose his job over this. He made a note of the media source, a local news reporter who had picked up the story from the medical crew that had taken Jamie to hospital. That reporter should know what happened to Mr Butler after his heroic deeds – then there *would* be a story to publish, thought Jamie. Yes, perhaps Mrs Jones would change her mind under some media pressure.

The idea seemed risky. Would Mr Butler end up in more trouble? But if he explained to the reporter that Mr Butler had willingly complied with Mrs Jones' demands that he leave the school, and that he knew nothing of Jamie's help in revealing the truth, then matters would not get worse for Mr Butler. They might indeed get worse for Jamie, but considering that Mr Butler had saved his life, it was the least he could do to try and reinstate Mr Butler at school.

Jamie hesitated before he began to compose a message to the local news reporter.

## Chapter 27

# Media Ignition

"You'd better come and look at this," said Alf#1 to Alf#2.

A news report had just been broadcast updating the sports day incident: *And following on from the heroic acts of school teacher, Mr Butler, we have learned from Jamie Parkinson that he has been forced out of the school by the head teacher, Mrs Jones. Mystery surrounds the reason why Mr Butler should be treated like this. We have requested an interview with Mrs Jones to clarify the reason he has allegedly lost his job following dramatic events at the school sports day ...*

"Oh my goodness," said Louisa#2, "Looks like Jamie has taken matters into his own hands!"

"He certainly has," said Alf#2, "I must say that Jamie is quite a proactive student."

*

The next morning a group of reporters were clamouring to request an interview with Mrs Jones at the school entrance. Mrs Jones peered out of her office window at the media frenzy. Jamie was standing quietly in her office – he had been summoned first thing to explain his actions. "What on earth were you thinking of Jamie?" she said, "Contacting a news reporter about Mr Butler! I told you yesterday that he left for personal reasons."

She looked like she might explode at any minute. "I went to see Mr Butler, and he told me the truth" said Jamie, almost at a whisper.

"The truth? I'll give them the truth. Now get out of my office you meddling boy!"

Jamie made a hasty retreat as Mrs Jones organised a meeting with the reporters. Instead of bending under media pressure it appeared that Mrs Jones had actually snapped.

*

"Mrs Jones, first of all I'd like to thank you for agreeing to speak to us so promptly" said the reporter. "We just need to clear up some details regarding allegations that Mr Butler was forced to resign from his teaching post at the school. Is there any truth in this?"

Mrs Jones waited for the chattering reporters to become silent as though she were at a class assembly. "I am sorry to say that these allegations are completely … true." She had almost opted to deny the allegations, but at that precise moment she had decided once and for all to come clean. There was excited mutterings among the reporters gathered in the meeting room.

"And for what reason did you find it necessary to force Mr Butler to resign?" asked a reporter sensing that there might be more in this story than he had anticipated.

"Do you really want to know why I could not tolerate Mr Butler in this school any longer?" she asked.

"Er, yes please", said a reporter just in case she needed prompting.

"It's because he is a… a ….

"No!" shouted a young voice at the back of the room. It was Jamie Parkinson. This was not what he wanted. She was supposed to reinstate Mr Butler – not reveal his true identity to the rest of the world. There were annoyed shushing sounds coming from the reporters eager to know what Mrs Jones had been about to say.

"I'm sorry Jamie," said Mrs Jones "You wanted the truth – well I'm not keeping this quiet any longer - this is the truth ladies and gentlemen. Mr Butler is a … Transapient."

There was a stunned silence – this was way beyond a cat-stuck-up-a-tree story that they usually had to deal with. Most of the reporters were unfamiliar with the term; some thought it was something to do with a sex change. One of the reporters had come across the term when covering a science and technology conference the previous year, so he broke the silence with the next question.

"Do you mean to say that he is a sentient machine, able to think for himself?" he asked.

"Exactly," said Mrs Jones, she was tempted to award him a house point, but checked herself – these were not school children, they were adults with the ability to shine a media spotlight on anything they observed and raise awareness across the world.

Then, as if a dam across comprehension had been lifted, a torrent of questions came forth, each competing with the adjacent question by raising the volume one more notch. The result was an unintelligible loud babble of earnest voices.

Mrs Jones raised both hands as if repelling the noise, and gradually the questions subsided as they waited for her to speak – this was her school – she was in control. "Now, ladies and gentlemen, if you would just like to raise your hands, I will take questions … one at a time." Order had been established once more, they had all mentally regressed to their childhood, complying with the authoritative figure of the head teacher, as she pointed to a random reporter.

"How did you first find out Mr Butler was a … er, Transopient?" he asked.

“The term is ‘Transapient’,” she corrected him. The reporter cringed and nodded in acknowledgement of his error.

“Mr Butler is based on his human predecessor who worked here for the last eight years,” she explained. “This transapient has been derived from his body – the human Mr Butler died a few months ago. This, this machine has been impersonating Mr Butler in our school as some sort of experiment, and I fear for the safety of our children. That is why I asked the transapient Mr Butler to leave.” She pointed to the next questioner.

“Can we speak to Mr Butler?” he asked sensing the scoop of a lifetime a few questions away.

“He does not work at this school anymore.” Mrs Jones could feel the attention of all the reporters was now shifting away from her; they were all sensing the potential interview of the century.

“Can you tell us where he lives?” This question was unnecessary. Alf’s address was not a public secret and could be found in a few seconds on the hypernet.

“I’m sorry, I cannot give you teacher’s details,” replied Mrs Jones. Jamie watched aghast at the back of the room – *well you have certainly divulged enough other important details of his teacher* he thought to himself. I must warn Mr Butler.

Jamie left the meeting which was descending into chaos again as each reporter became impatient to have their question answered. He quickly composed a message to Alf#2:

*URGENT: Mrs Jones has gone public. News reporters will be after you soon. Sorry. Jamie*

## Chapter 28

# In the Spotlight

Dr Roberts stared at the news report that had flashed up as she worked in the laboratory at ABC-Tech. "Oh no – it's happened sooner than I would have hoped."

The story of the possible existence of a transapient teacher had spread rapidly to national news reporters. Some media outlets were hedging their bets, speculating that this was probably some kind of hoax since little corroborative evidence had been presented. However, this speculation was raising the interest in transapient technology and Dr Roberts was already receiving enquiries from various academic sources asking about the maturity of transapient technology. She ignored the messages and quickly called up the transapients who were at home viewing the same media reports in dismay. This was far too soon for them all. Their anonymity would surely disappear as the whole world clamoured to view this new lifeform.

Alf#2 activated the holophone and Dr Roberts appeared among them all. "I see you are up to speed with developments," noted Dr Roberts. "We all knew this would go public eventually. If you want to come to the laboratory we can provide security barriers to prevent the media from …"

"No thanks," said Alf#2. "We put a lot of effort into achieving our liberty and independence, and much as we all appreciate what you have done for us, we would rather face the music in our own home."

There were already a group of reporters standing at the entrance to their home, peering in trying to catch a glimpse of the elusive transapient. The three Louisas and two Alfs had already locked all the outer doors to prevent any reporter from barging their way into their home.

"Okay, I admire your determination to carry on," said Dr Roberts. "But let me know if you need any help."

"We might take you up on that," said Louisa, who felt as though their home was suddenly under siege.

Floods of messages were now being received with all sorts of offers for publication rights. Some of the media were betting that unlikely as it seemed, if transapients did exist, they wanted to be the first to access this story – the emergence of a new lifeform – the evolutionary step for mankind – the event of the century.

"As far as I can make out, it would appear that nobody yet knows about the other transapients, only Alf#2," noted Dr Roberts. "You haven't mentioned their existence to Jamie have you?" she asked Alf#2.

"No, I haven't", said Alf#2. "I only revealed my own identity because he became suspicious about me straight away."

"Good," said Dr Roberts. "Now, it may be better in the long run to give them one interview so they do not dig around too much by themselves. How would you feel about that?"

"Okay, but in our own time," said Alf#1 defiantly. "We will not be put on parade at a moment's notice."

"I understand," said Dr Roberts. "Would you like me to liaise with the media on your behalf, it might be more manageable; we have a team here who deal with public relations." The five looked at each other and all nodded their agreement.

"Perhaps you could persuade the hoard on our doorstep to give us a bit of privacy?" asked Louisa.

"I'll do my best," answered Dr Roberts. At least she now had an extremely large carrot to dangle in front of the media spotlight.

*

Later that evening, somehow the doorstep reporters had been persuaded to retreat some distance away. They were sure to be watching the house like hawks, ready to swoop and snap up any factual snippets that may emerge from the house of mystery. The local neighbourhood were already being interviewed at length – trying to glean as much information about the Butlers as possible. There was no official record of Alf Butler's death – so some of them began to dismiss the story as an elaborate hoax. Others had found out that Louisa's sister and husband were staying at their home. But records showed that Louisa did not have a sister. Who then was this mysterious couple?

Louisa sighed. "I know you transapients do not need to eat or sleep, but I'm afraid I do. Would anyone like to pop out and get me some food?" she asked. She could not bear to face the barrage of sensor equipment that had been set up outside their house during the day.

"I'll go," said Louisa#2. "They should not know that I am a transapient – maybe they will let me through without too much fuss."

Louisa#2 opened the door. Powerful telephoto lenses were trained on the front entrance in case anybody decided to leave the house. "It's the wife," hissed one reporter monitoring an array of imagery covering most of the exit points around the house. Louisa#2 had barely walked a few steps before her path was blocked by eager reporters asking rapid fire questions. A security team drafted in from

ABC-Tech had also anticipated this confrontation, and quickly established a human shield around Louisa#2.

Louisa#2 stopped to face the reporters, more confident now she had some protection. Meanwhile inside the house Alf#2 and the others were watching the live stream of the confrontation which was being broadcast across the hypernet as breaking news, such was the immediacy of news afforded by hypernet coverage.

“Good evening everyone.” The clamour of questions stopped as they waited, ears and microphones straining to pick up every utterance from this, the wife of the first transapient. “I know this may be a bit of an anti-climax to some of you, but I am just popping out to get some food. I have nothing else to say – as you know there will be an official interview shortly. Good night.”

One reporter persisted with questions “When will that be, Mrs Butler?” he demanded, trying to block her path.

“You heard the lady!” said a gruff man from the security team as he and his colleagues forged a path through the mass of disgruntled reporters who now sensed that this would not be their night.

“That’s my girl,” said Alf#2 and Alf#1 together.

“I never knew I had it in me!” laughed Louisa as she watched Louisa#2 battle her way towards the local food store.

## Chapter 29

# The Interview

Several days passed in which the reporters realized there would be no exclusive interviews on offer. A time and venue for the interview had been set by Dr Roberts based solely on the preferences of Alf#2 and his household. This had given the reporters and their team of researchers more time to dig into Alf and Louisa's background – a normal couple but with one or two anomalies surrounding their lives.

Finally the day of questioning arrived. A press release had been published that day by ABC-Tech which confirmed that they were responsible for creating a transapient based on Alf Butler and the fact that they were allowed to release him into human society under approved licence agreements, which were appended to the press release pack. Alf#2 and Louisa#2 sat with Dr Roberts and awaited questions from the packed lecture theatre at ABC-Tech.

Alf#1, Louisa and Louisa#2 stayed at home to watch a live stream of the interview along with millions of other viewers. There was still some doubt as to the authenticity of the claim that a transapient had been created, so viewing figures were not quite as high as they could have been, many were viewing in the hope that it was true rather than a sophisticated publicity stunt. Now at last the alleged new being was in front of them to be scrutinized in this one off interview.

"Mr Alf Butler, on behalf of all humans, welcome to our world", said the first interviewer, his tone suggesting some doubt over his alleged status.

"Thank you," said Alf#2. "As a direct descendant of a human donor, I believe I have the moral right to share 'your' world." The room was suddenly silent as Alf#2 spoke. His immediate challenge to the first interviewer's welcome was unexpected.

"Forgive us for being sceptical Mr Butler, but could you prove to us that you are really a transapient rather than a human professing to be one," asked the first interviewer immediately going on the offensive. He did not like the quick response from his opening introduction.

"That is not as easy as it sounds," said Alf#2.

"Really?" said the first interviewer smirking suspiciously.

"Yes, you see I have scored one hundred percent in all Turing tests – tests designed to differentiate me from human beings. So we could talk until the middle of next week and you would not be able to distinguish me from a human."

"That is assuming you are not already a human," countered the first interviewer.

"Yes, we need to establish that my body is not based on organic tissue," said Alf#2.

Another interviewer raised his hand to speak, "Mr Butler would you object to undergoing a live comparative bio-scan? It just so happens I have bought along my own, just in case"

"Now? Of course I have no objections," said Alf#2.

"Excellent" said the second interviewer eagerly; surprised that Mr Butler was so willing to undergo this level of scrutiny. "We just need another volunteer as a human representative. How about your wife?"

"It's okay Louisa," interjected Dr Roberts. "You have been through enough over the last few days. I will volunteer as the human representative."

Alf#1, Louisa and Louisa#2 heaved a collective sigh of relief, thankful to Dr Roberts for her swift intervention. The bio-scan comparison between two transapients was not what was needed at that moment.

The reporter with the bio-scan equipment made his way to the front of the room and passed the scanner around Dr Roberts' body. A holographic projection of Dr Roberts' body organs was displayed within a three dimensional image which gradually rotated around a vertical axis, so that transparent views of her skeleton and organs were visible to everyone in the packed meeting room, as well as being available as a live broadcast on the hypernet.

A list of elements was also shown by percentage indicating typical proportions for human composition: 65% Oxygen, 18.5% Carbon, 8.5% Hydrogen, 3.2% Nitrogen, 1.5% Calcium, 1.0% Phosphorus, 0.4% Potassium, 0.3% Sulphur, 0.2% Sodium, 0.2%, Chlorine, 0.1% Magnesium and 1% various other trace elements. Dr Roberts surveyed herself – and checked through the list, relieved to see no abnormal levels. "This is definitely a human composition," announced the second interviewer, just in case anyone was in any doubt.

"Just as I suspected," said Dr Roberts. There were a few grunts of acknowledgement around the room.

"And now for you Mr Butler." The bio-scanner was passed around Alf#2's body. The scan revealed a synthetic framework, but it immediately looked too regular to be a human skeleton. There was no alimentary canal, no stomach, no lungs, and no heart. The head contained a three dimensional array of billions of microscopic processing elements interconnected by a fine mesh of fibres, which trailed down the spine and split off across the body, just like human nerves. Some of the material looked as though it served no purpose except to help present human contours to an external observer.

And then the list of elements appeared: 5% Oxygen, 73% Carbon, 0.5% Hydrogen, 14.6% Silicon, … the list went on to include a wide range of chemicals found in synthetic materials.

Alf#2 looked at the image with interest, the rest of the room and those around the world receiving the hypernet broadcast looked in stunned silence at the composition of Alf#2. The second interviewer was lost for words as he tried to make sense of what he was seeing. Finally he recovered enough composure to announce, "Mr Butler, you are an android!"

Alf#2 was pleased that his non-human identity had been confirmed by a third party. "I am more than an android," said Alf#2. "I am a sentient being with independent thoughts, as human as yours. In fact I am aware of all Alf Butler's human experiences to such an extent that from my perspective I am Alf Butler".

As the interview progressed viewing figures around the world gradually increased as the news of the interview, which appeared to confirm the existence of a transapient, spread like an informational tsunami.

The second interviewer returned to his seat, still in shock at what he had revealed. He had been expecting to show that Alf#2 was human and hence part of an elaborate hoax.

The mood in the room had changed. Everyone now wanted to know more details about what it was like to be a transapient, what did his wife think of her new husband and how he had managed to be a full time teacher for several months without being recognised as a different being to his human predecessor.

Eventually one reporter, who after much digging around had become aware of various anomalous details associated with the Butler's background, raised his hand to ask a question.

“Mrs Butler, is it difficult to cope with two babies as well as a transapient?” The question came as a surprise to many who knew Louisa and particularly to Louisa#2, facing the question. A few milliseconds of processing were needed to postulate that the reporter had found birth certificates registered by Louisa related to the two transapient models to provide official identities for the transapients of Louisa and Alf#1

“But I do not have any children,” said Louisa#2. It was the only response she could think of that could possibly deflect from the truth.

“Really?” said the third interviewer slowly. “But there are two births registered under your name in the last month. Adam Butler born on 23$^{rd}$ April 2059, and Eve Butler born on 2$^{nd}$ August 2059. It seems unlikely that two children could be born to the same mother only four months apart. And another point that seems a bit odd. Who is the lady staying with you reported to be your sister – you do not have a sister do you.” This was another fact which he had confirmed by official records. The interviewer had been doing his homework.

“I repeat,” said Louisa#2, “I do not have any children and I am not willing to discuss the personal information of my house guests – that is a private matter for them.”

Everyone sensed that there was something odd going on but no one could identify how the two anomalies fitted together, until the next question reared its head. “Dr Roberts, would you like to explain why ABC-Tech’s license agreement was amended to allow more than one transapient to be released into human society?”

Dr Roberts felt as though the interviewing pack were moving in for the kill. She knew that registering the transapients as humans would increase the chance of revealing the transapients’ identities, but she had never thought that it would be in such a public arena with millions of viewers hanging on her response.

"After the probationary period of Alf Butler's transapient," said Dr Roberts, "we felt confident that he did not pose a threat to human society. We therefore had the licence changed in anticipation of the release of more transapients."

"And have you released more transapients?" pressed the third interviewer.

Dr Roberts hesitated before she answered "Yes." It was no use denying the facts – they were clearly on the trail of the other transapients. There was a murmur of interest within the room. Not only was there this transapient before them, but there were others around too.

"Would these other transapients happen to include Louisa's mysterious sister?" The third interviewer was so close to the truth – but the one thing he had not worked out was that the mysterious sister was in fact the human Louisa, and that the Mrs Louisa Butler he was currently interviewing was Louisa's transapient and not human.

"My 'mysterious sister' is not a transapient" said Louisa#2 with total conviction – it was the truth, and the interviewer's confidence about his conclusion was suddenly in doubt.

A fourth interviewer raised his hand "Dr Roberts, can you tell us the identity of these extra transapients? Don't you think we have a right to know? If it had not been for the bio-scan then you could be a transapient and we would never know the difference."

Dr Roberts looked sternly back at the fourth interviewer. "Transapients are a directly descended from humans – as such, I believe they should have the same rights of privacy as any human being. Whether or not they choose to make themselves known should be their decision and I am not willing to betray their confidence."

The fourth interviewer had seen the revelation made by Mrs Jones and knew that a proportion of the general public, Mrs Jones being a prime example, would be uncomfortable living alongside these man-made beings – technophobia would be taken to a new level. “I think that many people will want to know whether they are talking to a human or a human imitation,” said the fourth interviewer.

Something stirred within Louisa#2. It was time to put an end to this pretence. “Are you comfortable talking to me?” she was turning the tables and now asking the questions in the interview. Dr Roberts looked at Louisa in surprise at the question.

“Well, yes. Of course I am,” said the fourth interviewer. “You’re Mrs Butler, the wife of the late Alfred Butler,” he said as though stating the obvious.

“Am I?” she asked. “Perceptions can be deceptive you know. How can you be so sure?” Louisa#2 beckoned the reporter with the bio-scan equipment to come forward. After a moment, the reporter obliged and made his way to the front of the room once more. Louisa#2 spread her arms, presenting herself for elementary analysis. The resulting image and element proportions were identical to Alf#2. Everyone gasped in astonishment, including the growing millions of viewers around the world.

“I don’t believe it!” cried Jamie who was watching his teacher from home, glued to the unfolding dramatic interview.

“Thank you for your words of support,” said Louisa#2 publicly to Dr Roberts. It was her endorsement of transapients rights which had precipitated her need to stand up and be counted.

The third interviewer, who had incorrectly identified Louisa’s ‘mysterious sister’ as a transapient, now reached the correct conclusion about her identity – she was the human Louisa. He raised his arm again to confirm his thoughts, just in case there were any more twists, “Am I correct in deducing that the ‘mysterious sister’ is the human Mrs Butler, and that the two registered births are for the transapient Mr and Mrs Butler?”

Alf#2, Louisa#2 and Dr Roberts all nodded. They were also all thinking the same thing. The existence of Alf#1 and Louisa#1 had escaped the media magnifying glass that had found two transapients. Their transapient twins Alf#1 and Louisa#1, and Louisa were all at home watching events with empathy, recognising what Louisa#2 had done. “You can be proud of your self,” said Alf#2 with a grin.

## Chapter 30

# Goodbye Alf

Now that their true identities were known to the public, it was possible to officially say goodbye to the human Alf. A funeral was soon arranged, but unfortunately this also attracted much media attention. The strange sight of Alf#2 attending his own funeral created much public interest. Alf's spirit had been preserved in Alf#2 and so his 'being' had not died totally; he had migrated his spirit to a new body and achieved an existence which was potentially immortal. His digitised self could be preserved, copied and protected; binary states had no concept of time.

Alf#1 and Louisa sat among the many people who had come to Alf's funeral, and listened as Alf#2 gave a reflective account of his own life up to his own death. He was fully aware of Alf's memories and was able to give accurate first-hand accounts of his childhood and his later experiences as he grew up, eventually becoming a teacher at Jamie's school.

When he described how he first met Louisa he could not help but look towards her. At the time they knew straight away that they would be together eternally. A tear trickled down Louisa's cheek as she relived the life she had shared with Alf. She knew that the Alf talking to them about himself was not physically the same person, but the way he talked and related their shared past made him indistinguishable from her human Alf. To her it was as though he had never died.

Jamie was also finding it very difficult to accept that Mr Butler had died. He had witnessed the seamless transition from human to transapient at school and could hardly tell the difference. Indeed, he was the only person in the school who had suspected there was something different about the transapient Alf. At the end of the service Jamie went over to Alf#2 and shook his hand. He was glad that his teacher had confided in him, and still felt guilty about playing his part in revealing his identity to the wider world. Alf#2 seemed to know what Jamie was thinking. "I'm glad our existence is now public knowledge, Jamie," said Alf#2. "We don't have to hide ourselves away any more, and it has allowed us to say goodbye to the human Alf."

"You have not died as far as I'm concerned," said Jamie. "You have just moved on to a new life."

Alf#2 nodded. "Thanks Jamie," he said.

Dr Roberts came over to Alf#2; she looked at Alf's coffin and then back to Alf#2. "Thanks for telling us all about Alf," she said. "I never met you before you became a transapient – it was good to hear about your previous life. It must have felt strange giving your own eulogy."

"Yes it was," agreed Alf#2. "I was not sure whether to use 'I', 'we', or 'he' when describing Alf's life. It definitely feels like it should be 'I' to me."

"If it feels like 'I', then I am pleased; it was always my ambition to make a sentient being," said Dr Roberts. "You are a living testament to Alf. Not only should we celebrate his human life, but we should also celebrate the birth of his new transapient life."

"I agree," said Louisa#2. "I think we should definitely have transapient birthdays".

Louisa joined the group. She had been thinking about the human Alf and trying hard to separate him in her mind from the transapient Alf. "That was a lovely review of your life," said Louisa as she hugged

Alf#2. She knew he was different, and yet he was the same within. He believed he was Alf, and if it were not for the differences in his body chemistry, he would never have known there was a difference.

"Come on, let's go home," said Alf#2. They battled their way through the waiting reporters, all eager to ask insensitive questions. This was not the time for a press conference and the media had to be satisfied with video footage of the service as a record of this unusual funeral.

*

When they got home they were greeted by Alf#1 and Louisa#1 who had followed the funeral on a hypernet stream. Alf#1 could see that Alf#2 had been struggling to come to terms with Alf's human funeral. "He is definitely pleased with the funeral," said Alf#1 reassuringly. "It was uncanny to hear our life being described; just as I remember it too." The two Alf's had identical recollections about their human life, being derived from identical brain state matrices.

The three Louisas had a group hug. Their mutual feelings did not need to be expressed in any other way; they all felt the same about Alf. The Alf that they had all known was gone, but identical Alfs had taken his place.

Through know intent of their own the interview and subsequently Alf's funeral had made the transapients sensational topics of the hypernet. There were still some who thought that they could well be an elaborate hoax. One suggestion was that the illusion of a sentient being could be made by a remotely controlled android avatar. Although technically feasible this suggestion was strongly denied by ABC-Tech.

The transapients were not concerned by such speculation. As far as they were concerned, their status was now publicly recognised; they were now officially classified as new sentient beings.

## Chapter 31

# Star Dust Settles

As far as the world was concerned there was now a transapient couple; the husband transapient based on a dead human, the wife transapient based on a living human. The media speculation about this triangle of beings went on for several days. It had nearly overshadowed the major revelation that a transapient had been created in the first place. The media was patting itself on the back for revealing the identities of the two transapients, so much so that nobody questioned who the partner of the human Louisa was.

Mrs Jones was horrified when she had watched the unveiling of another transapient. Where would this all end? Would everyone want a transapient version of themselves? Would the weaker humans gradually fade away as the efficient transapient offspring took over the world?

Mrs Jones' thoughts were not shared by Alf#2 and Louisa#2, who were just glad that the previous week's interview was behind them, half the truth was out, and maybe the media would lose interest when transapients became yesterday's news. An essence of Mrs Jones thoughts was shared by Dr Roberts. She still felt like a mother in some sense to the transapients; she was after all their creator, and this gave her many maternal thoughts regarding the protection of the transapients' future.

Her plans to this end were evolving in her mind. Who would look out for the transapients when she herself died? It was probably many years in the future, but she could not be sure, and the thought of her transapient children being left without their 'mother' was unsettling.

But there was a way of preserving herself - she was the one person with all the capability to do it. She could donate herself to a transapient Dr Roberts. Her expertise and more importantly her relationship with the transapients would be preserved. The idea when it came was totally seductive – she would become immortal through her own creation.

*

Meanwhile, at the International Space Agency's headquarters, Steve Bradshaw was mulling over the transapient's capabilities after digesting the previous week's interview along with the millions of other hypernet viewers. Steve had been involved with the International Space Agency (ISA) for many years, working on advanced projects aimed at space exploration. He had seen humans gradually migrating to various bodies within the solar system, but his thoughts and associated development projects were drawn to more ambitious destinations; destinations beyond the solar system to neighbouring stars – ultimately to neighbouring galaxies. The frailty of humans for these expeditions had always been a significant problem.

The nearest star systems were typically ten thousand times the distance to the gas giants of the solar system. In fact even travelling at the speed of light it would take more than four years to reach the nearest neighbouring star system. Robotic missions were always the practical way to explore other worlds; they would be used for lengthy and possibly risky reconnaissance missions to identify sites for potential future colonisation. But transapients with their human qualities would be able to respond to nearly every situation intelligently and represent humans as pioneering space explorers; they would experience the expedition first hand. We could certainly harness this technology, he thought as he ticked off the benefits in his mind.

The agency had recently developed a constant thrust propulsion system for their first interstellar mission. This would accelerate a spaceship continually during the first half of its voyage and decelerate by the same amount in the second half. For humans this would be the typically one g, providing a comfortable weight equivalent to earthbound gravity. But transapients should be able to take much larger accelerations – he needed to discuss this with ABC-Tech as soon as possible. This itself could prove to be a problem, as the publicity department of ABC-Tech would be inundated with requests for information following the interview.

Perhaps he should try to contact the transapients directly – they were after all being given the liberty to make their own decisions.

# Chapter 32

# I Think, Therefore You Are

It was 21st September 2059. Her eyes flickered open and she looked up at Dr Roberts. The last thing she could remember was working at the laboratory and hooking herself up to the molecular brain matrix scanner and closing her eyes as the complete state of her brain at that point in time was captured. That's right, it was coming back to her. She was having a molecular brain scan in order to create another transapient; this time of herself, she would be called Amelia#1.

"Hello Dr Roberts," said Dr Roberts. "How are you feeling?"

She looked up at … herself. Was she looking into a mirror? Well, herself seemed to be moving about independently, so maybe not. Was it a holographic projection?

Then after a few more moments while her brain completed initialisation routines, she knew why she was confused; she must be the transapient. "I feel … fine," she said intrigued to finally know what it was like to be her own creation. "So am I Amelia#1 or have you been up to your old tricks making more than one of me?" she asked.

"If you don't count me, there is only one of you so far," said Dr Roberts.

Just then the door began to open; it was Dr James. Dr Roberts darted to the door before he managed to open it completely. "Dr Roberts, you're working late again this evening. Is everything okay?" he asked. "I thought I heard voices."

"Everything's fine" said Dr Roberts. "I was just talking … to my self," she smiled at the intentional ambiguity in her statement. Dr James shook his head "You're working too hard – you should give yourself a break".

"Don't worry, I intend to," she said as Dr James headed off down the corridor.

When she was sure that they would not be disturbed again, Dr Roberts went back to her transapient self. "Your jokes don't get any better," noted Amelia#1. "Now let's get on with the functional tests," she commanded.

"Who do you think you are?" said Dr Roberts "Telling me what to do!"

"You of course," taunted Amelia#1. She knew that from now on she would be at least one step ahead of her creator. It was not Dr Robert's original intention, but now Amelia#1 realised that she had inherited her creator's ability to create – that could come in very useful indeed.

The next four hours were spent going through all the transapient tests needed to verify correct operation of Amelia#1. Dr Roberts was reduced to a redundant observer, since Amelia#1 was well aware of each test and what needed to be checked and recorded. At the end of the testing session Amelia#1 proudly announced, "Pleased to report, Dr Roberts, that apart from our slightly obsessive characteristics, all functions appear to be operating nominally."

"Good, now we just have to smuggle you out of here," said Dr Roberts looking at the time. It was very late; everyone else had left the building. There was only the security guard sitting at the main entrance to get past. Luckily he had already started to doze, but as Dr Roberts approached his desk he awoke immediately and pretended to be peering at one of the instruments that was clearly working normally. He nodded as she went past, “Good night, Dr Roberts.”

She smiled at him and stopped just out of sight as Amelia#1 waited for her chance. Sure enough only a few minutes passed before the security guard began to nod off again. Despite his shift work he could never get used to sleeping during the day.

Amelia#1 made a dash for it as Dr Roberts beckoned to her frantically just outside the main entrance. As she passed his desk he awoke again and rubbed his eyes. “Dr Roberts?” he said. “I thought I saw your double walk past here just now.”

“It’s okay,” said Amelia#1. “I forgot to turn off the laboratory lie detector.”

“Very funny, Dr Roberts,” yawned the puzzled security guard. He decided that he must have been dreaming. Dr Roberts had never joked like that in all the years she’d been there. “Good night,” he added as she strolled out of the main entrance.

Dr Roberts knew she should have gone through all the official channels to seek approval for the release of a third transapient, but she could not bear the thought of being prevented from seeing this one through. In some ways she felt like she’d achieved her life’s ambition and now it was time to pass that life’s experience on to her transapient. Her transapient had similar ideas.

They both knew where they were going. It was time to pay a visit to their fellow transapients at Alf and Louisa’s home. To avoid too much unwanted attention they took separate autonomous vehicles. Dr Roberts arrived first and made her way to the front entrance.

“It’s Dr Roberts”, Alf#1 called to the others. “At last, it’s someone who is not going to put us under a microscope.”

"I don't want to disappoint you," said Dr Roberts with a smile as she walked in to greet everyone, "but I've already seen you all in the smallest detail imaginable during your design. Anyway, how are you all coping with your new found fame?"

"Well," said Louisa#2, "it appears that Louisa#1 and Alf#1 have still not yet found the limelight."

"That's good news," said Dr Roberts, "and are you still out of work", she asked Alf#2.

"Yes, I am, but we have had some interesting offers…" began Alf#2, but he was interrupted by Alf#1.

"Hang on one second, there is someone else at the front entrance. You are not going to believe who it is!" Alf#1 looked at the familiar figure standing patiently exactly where Dr Roberts had stood a few moments earlier.

"Dr Roberts?" chorused everyone.

"Oh, I forgot to mention," said the Dr Roberts who was already in the house, "I have been a bit busy in the laboratory over the last couple of days working on a bit of private self-indulgence."

"So we see!" said Alf#1. "So tell us, which one of you is the transapient?"

"She is", said the two Dr Roberts together, pointing at each other.

"My transapient seems to have developed my sense of humour", laughed Dr Roberts.

"Oh go on then, it's me," admitted Amelia#1 performing a dainty pirouette on her heels.

"Welcome to the home for famous and unknown transapients," said Louisa. For once she was not the sole human in the house.

"Alf#1 was just about to tell me about some interesting offers they have received," Dr Roberts said to Amelia#1.

"Oh yes," said Alf#1. "Well the most interesting one by far is from someone at ISA, who would like to come and discuss possible help with one of their advanced projects."

"That does sound interesting," said Dr Roberts. "Did he give any details?"

"No," said Alf#1. "He wants to arrange a meeting to discuss details with all of us. In particular he would like to talk to Dr Roberts about some ideas he has."

"Okay," said Dr Roberts, "This is a chance for you to test your skills at being me," said Dr Roberts to Amelia#1.

"Can't wait," said Amelia#1 brightly. "I'll arrange a meeting for next week".

"Be careful what you agree to," said Dr Roberts, but she had complete confidence in her transapient creation, who in turn had complete confidence in her own abilities.

## Chapter 33

# Another Giant Leap?

Amelia#1 arranged the meeting at ABC-Tech and made sure that the minimum number of people were informed to avoid unwanted media attention. ABC-Tech saw this as potentially good publicity for transapients, and since they had already granted them independence, they merely asked to be kept informed of any developments.

Steve Bradshaw arrived in good spirits. He was pleased that the transapients had responded positively to his suggestion for this meeting. He wondered how they would react to his proposal for their involvement. He kept having to remind himself that the transapients were man-made, but as they were sentient beings they had somehow transcended the cold mechanical predictability of processing androids.

"Welcome to the Advanced Bio Computing Technology Centre," said Amelia#1. "I am Dr Roberts, and this is Mr and Mrs Butler, the first transapients to be created"

"Thank you for inviting me here and giving me the opportunity to talk to you about some exciting projects we are involved in." Steve could not help studying Alf#2 and Louisa#2 who were both avoiding the temptation to correct Amelia#1; the fact was they were both the second transapients to be created. "First of all I'd like to tell you ~~know~~ about some research projects ISA has been undertaking over the last few years, where we are at the moment and what we could achieve with your involvement".

A holographic projection of the solar system appeared in front of them initially showing the planets out to Mars together with their main moons. "As you know, ISA have gradually been setting up colonies throughout our solar system. Our moon was the first step less than one hundred years ago." The holographic projection zoomed around the surface of the moon showing a number of settlements which were now small cities used for scientific study and holiday resorts. "Mars was the next site to be explored with the first human visitors in 2029. With improvements in space technology we went on to establish outposts on several moons of the gas giants in the following two decades." The holographic projection proceeded with a quick tour of the outer solar system and the asteroid mining craft extracting material for more construction projects; it was efficient to extract material from this resource rather than expending vast amounts of energy launching massive structures directly from Earth. This was all familiar history to all those assembled at the meeting, but was an essential introduction to set the scene for Steve's propositions.

"But the solar system is not the end of space exploration; there are other worlds to explore orbiting distant stars – and herein lies the challenge," Steve paused while the projection zoomed out, the solar system shrinking to a dot dominated by the Sun. Eventually a star cluster appeared consisting of three stars, one of which was a red dwarf. "This is our nearest neighbour star system, Alpha Centauri, which is 4.24 light years from Earth, a significant jump in distance compared to our solar system – it's about ten thousand time more distant than our current sphere of exploration. The cluster consists of three stars; two are of similar size to the Sun while the third is a red dwarf about one eighth of the mass of the Sun. In 2016 an Earth like planet was discovered orbiting the red dwarf, Proxima Centauri, with the imaginative name of Proxima-B".

Louisa#2 found this amusing; fancy calling something with a letter suffix. She looked across to Alf#2 who somehow knew what Louisa#2 was thinking. Alf#2 sent her an optical text message

**** Louisa#B? No I think Louisa#2 suits you better ****

"This exoplanet has received considerable attention over the years," Steve continued. "In 2036 a set of tiny robotic craft were sent to survey Proxima Centauri – their results should start coming back next year as the craft arrived three years ago in 2056 and their data will start being received in 2060, as the messages take over four years to come back across the enormous distance. Which brings me back to the challenges of the endeavour to reach this remote star system. ISA have been developing an interstellar spacecraft called M2C which is capable of travelling at half the speed of light."

"But doesn't that need enormous amounts of energy?" asked Amelia#1.

"Yes, indeed," Steve replied. "It has been a major hurdle, but we now have a source of energy even more efficient than a fusion reactor, even more efficient than the sun's main source of energy."

"Antimatter?" said Amelia#1 quietly.

Steve was impressed that Dr Roberts had immediately uttered the solution. "Correct again Dr Roberts. The vast energy locked up in all matter from that famous equation $E = mc^2$ is most efficiently release by the annihilation of matter with antimatter.

"How do you make antimatter?" asked Alf#2. It sounded like a dangerous thing to do.

"Quark nuggets" said Amelia#1.

"Pardon?" said Alf#2. It sounded to him like a fast food energy source.

"Dr Roberts, you seem to know the solutions to all these problems already," said Steve. "It appears that you have a good knowledge of energy sources – would you like to pre-empt the location of quark nuggets."

"Certainly," said Amelia#1. "Quark nuggets are balls of dense superconducting quark matter that were created at the Quantum Chromo Dynamics phase transition in the first microseconds of the universe. They can be found today in the cores of planets and more conveniently in a number of asteroids. Stable nuggets have a diameter of a few millimeters and a mass of tens of megatons. The high energy particles radiating from these nuggets can be used to generate antimatter."

Alf#2, Louisa#2 and Steve stared at Amelia#1. "I'm pleased you are so conversant with this energy source, Dr Roberts," said Steve eventually. He had thought before the meeting that he would be most impressed by the transapients, rather than their creator. "Yes, quark nuggets are indeed locked up in small asteroids, and we have created antimatter production factories in the asteroid belt for the last five years. The antimatter created here will be used as fuel for the spacecraft's gamma ray laser propulsion system."

"So, how much antimatter would the spacecraft need?" asked Louisa#2.

"Well, our baseline mission assumes that the spacecraft accelerates continuously at one g for eight months, until it reaches half the speed of light. The propulsion would then be switched off for seven years cruising at this speed and covering 3.5 light years. Finally another eight months would be spent decelerating at minus one g. At these speeds the crew would only experience seven years for the whole trip taking into account relativistic time dilation. For this particular mission we will need 2.5 kilogram of antimatter fuel for every kilogram of dry spacecraft mass."

“That seems encouraging, considering that the early Apollo rockets had 18,488 kg of propellant to get three astronauts to the moon,” said Amelia#1.

Steve was impressed once more by Dr Roberts’ detailed knowledge of space travel. “Yes we are nearly ready for a robotic launch as soon as we hear back from the nanocraft reconnaissance mission next year. That will narrow down the possibilities for exploration of Proxima-B.”

“Thank you Mr Bradshaw for that fascinating overview of your current project,” said Ameila#1. “How can transapients help with this mission?” she asked, even though she had already guessed what Steve had in mind.

“Well, the interstellar bus M2C is ready for launch and I would like to offer your transapients a ticket to the stars.”

Chapter 34

# Interstellar Mission Update

"Is that a return ticket?" asked Louisa#2 sounding a bit worried.

"I'm afraid the design is one way," admitted Steve.

"But we don't need to get there that quick," stated Amelia#1. "If we switch off the propellant after four months we only need one kg of antimatter fuel for every kg of spacecraft mass. The outward journey time would be doubled to 14 years, and another 14 years for the return trip; transapients are not affected by the passage of time."

Steve's mission had originally been for dispensable equipment. There had never been a plan to actually return from Proxima-B. "Yes that would appear possible," he said slowly, again marvelling at Dr Roberts mental abilities. *How could she work out that solution so quickly?*

"Excellent," said Amelia#1. "One more question Mr Bradshaw."

"Er, yes?" Steve was still reeling from the sudden major tweak to the mission objectives; a return mission.

"I trust there is room for a third occupant?" she asked tentatively.

"Yes, as transapients do not need the life support overheads of humans, we can certainly accommodate three transapients… but I thought you had only made two."

"Indeed, *I* have only made two transapients, but I am thinking of a redundant third transapient for reliability."

Alf#2 and Louisa#2 immediately picked up on Amelia#1's intention. "We will need to set up working meetings with your project team to become fully integrated into the mission," said Amelia#1.

"So you are accepting the proposition?" asked Steve. "This is a great opportunity for a being to experience interstellar travel first hand."

"I will need to just check with my colleagues at ABC-Tech, but in principle I can't see why not," said Amelia#1 confidently.

Steve left the meeting feeling very positive about the outcome. A return journey opened up all sorts of possibilities – the media would be eager to follow the personal voyages of their human representatives heading off to new frontiers.

*

When Steve had left the meeting Louisa#2 looked concerned. "Do we get a say in this?" she asked. Although she was a transapient she still had the human feelings of apprehension.

"Of course," said Amelia#1. "The choice is absolutely yours – but I know that I for one will be going on this trip of a lifetime."

"But he doesn't know you are a transapient," said Louisa#2. "In fact no one knows, apart from us."

"I don't think Mr Bradshaw will mind a keen cosmologist like myself being in the crew – he seemed rather impressed don't you think?" she grinned.

"Well what do you think, Alf?" asked Louisa#2.

"I think it will be a fantastic adventure," said Alf#2. "Just you and me and the stars - how romantic!"

"Ahem," interjected Amelia#1. "Don't forget your transapient mother!"

They all laughed, and at that moment the decision as far as they were concerned had been made.

*

Later that evening Alf#2, Louisa#2 and Amelia#1 joined Alf#1, Louisa#1, Dr Roberts and Louisa to discuss the potential mission with ISA.

“So you will stow yourself away on an interstellar spaceship?” said Dr Roberts, who was not sure whether to be excited or worried about the prospect.

“Yes, we’ll be intrepid explorers, pushing back the frontiers for mankind, I can’t wait,” said Amelia#1 excitedly.

“But you won’t be back here for thirty years?” Louisa sighed; she could not quite comprehend waiting that long for their return.

“It is a long time,” agreed Dr Roberts. “But I think it’s a wonderful opportunity for transapients to show their capabilities. Transapients have the resilience to explore the stars on our behalf. One day Proxima-B might be a gateway to thousands of fascinating worlds that until now we have only known by indirect observations viewed through light years of space.”

“Couldn’t have put it better myself,” said Amelia#1

## Chapter 35

# Countdown to Lift-off

The following months saw intense activity as the project team at ISA adopted the new mission details. The spacecraft M2C was modified to create a space for the transapients to feel comfortable; this was more a psychological necessity inherited from their human persona as they actually were in need of minimal facilities.

The media had soon learnt that the transapients, who had only just become famous, were to form the crew of a mission to Proxima Centauri. Mrs Jones smiled to herself as she learned the news. She could not think of a better place to send the transapients – thirty years of transapient absence was music to her ears. Jamie on the other hand was beside himself with excitement over the prospect of his old maths teacher heading off on a space adventure.

There was some confusion about whether there would be two or three crew members. Since Amelia#1 had asked about a third space on the mission, Steve Bradshaw had just factored in a third member and thought that Dr Roberts would contact him when the third transapient was ready.

Details of the spacecraft design and operation were sent to ABC-Tech, where Dr Roberts arranged for the information to be uploaded to the transapients' storage subsystems. They would become experts in using the range of equipment on board the spacecraft which would normally take years to absorb.

Several months were spent in simulation environments to check that the transapients understood all the equipment that could be controlled or monitored under a wide range of trial conditions.

Somehow another transapient, Amelia#2 had been quietly created at ABC-Tech. Dr Roberts felt happier knowing there were two transapient versions of herself, just in case Amelia#1 failed to return. After Dr Roberts ensured that Amelia#2 had received the matrix updates of Amelia#1, she sent Amelia#2 to see Steve Bradshaw at the ISA operations centre to deliver a package for the transapients to take; Amelia#2 explained that it was the spare transapient platform which would act as a redundant back up if there were any problems with Alf#2 or Louisa#2. Steve arranged for the package to be stowed in the transapients living area. He was very busy making sure all the design updates were feasible and the package was simply assigned a storage area for transapient related equipment.

Eventually results were received from the nano spacecraft which had passed close to Proxima Centauri four years previously. This was headline news around the world; the first close up glimpse of an exoplanet which had previously been inferred by the faintest of wiggles in the star's position.

The images and telemetered measurements confirmed that as suspected Proxima-B was tidally locked to its parent star; one side was constantly exposed to the full glare of Proxima Centauri, the other hemisphere remaining in perpetual freezing darkness. This had resulted in a distinctive ring at the day to night boundary on the planet's surface with a tantalising dark green band visible within the day lit hemisphere. Nothing like this had been seen in the Sun's solar system, some 4.24 light years away.

The light from Proxima Centauri bathed the planet in a weak red glow. In the visible region of the spectrum the amount of light was only two percent of that received on Earth with most of the radiative flux from the red dwarf emitted in the infrared. As seen from Proxima-B the red dwarf host star appeared to be three times the diameter of the Sun viewed from Earth. Even though the red dwarf size is one eighth that of the Sun, its distance from the host star is only 7 million km (a twentieth of the distance between the Earth and Sun). At this distance the planet has year of only 11.168 days.

But the most significant measurement transmitted across the 40 trillion km distance was that the on board spectrometers had picked up the signatures of water vapour and ozone. The presence of ozone created a buzz of excitement back on Earth. This would mean Proxima-B's atmosphere comprised a large proportion of oxygen, typically associated with biological activity. To top this, the presence of a methane marker appeared to confirm that the planet could well be the site of some form of active extra-terrestrial life.

The news propelled the interstellar mission to the top of everyone's agenda as a wave of anticipation swept around the world. This interest was not even dampened when Steve Bradshaw had to explain that, yes, it would take fourteen years to get to the exoplanet and another four years to receive any news back from Proxima-B. The Earth bound inhabitants had grown so used to the immediacy of the hypernet; their patience was in short supply. *Can we not get there any faster?* they would ask. Steve had to point out that only a few decades previously the trip would have taken 70,000 years using primitive rocket propellant. Until recently, before antimatter production had become feasible as a spacecraft fuel, the mission length would have been well beyond a human's lifetime; technological advances had reduced this to two decades; a remarkable achievement.

And so it was on a grey autumnal day that all the transapients except a conspicuously missing Amelia#1, gathered together to say their farewells to Alf#2 and Louisa#2. "Don't forget to unpack the third crew member" Amelia#2 reminded the two intrepid astronauts.

Louisa#1 and Louisa#2 regarded each other with a mixture of envy and admiration. Dr Roberts was reminded of the twin paradox in which identical twins are separated when one twin heads off in a spaceship travelling at relativistic speeds. Time for the travelling twin slows down significantly at speeds approaching the speed of light. When the twin returns their chronological age is different as they have aged at different rates. For the transapients travelling at one third the speed of light the age difference would amount to 18 months. For higher speeds or longer distances the age difference would be larger, but since the transapients showed no signs of visible aging their age difference would not be noticeable.

Dr Roberts and Louisa, however would be nearly thirty years older mainly because of the long journey time regardless of any relativistic time dilation.

With promises to keep in touch with regular updates they watched Alf#2 and Louisa#2 head off to their first stage of their immense journey; a space jet scheduled to leave for rendezvous with M2C the following day. “Don’t worry,” said Amelia#2 to Dr Roberts. “They are ideally suited to this mission. They need no food, no oxygen and will not suffer from fatigue. They will come back one day with tales to tell.” Amelia#2 would also one day be able to retrospectively experience the whole mission by updating her brain matrix with Amelia#1’s experiences throughout the trip.

## Chapter 36

# Earth Orbit

The ISA launch site was packed with spectators and media reporters, all eager to witness the start of an epic voyage. The sight of two figures strolling out hand in hand to the space jet was being beamed around the world – the transapients were now international heroes representing the humans in a quest of space exploration. Louisa glanced at Alf#1 as they viewed the historic scene – reaching out to hold his hand echoing the connection between the transapient astronauts they were watching.

The scene then cut to an interview with Dr Roberts and Steve Bradshaw who had made themselves available to field a barrage of questions from reporters. "And we are joined now by Dr Roberts, responsible for the creation of the first transapient beings, and Steve Bradshaw, responsible for this ambitious interstellar space mission; the exploration of our closest neighbour star Proxima Centauri and its associated exoplanet, Proxima B. Dr Roberts, you must be very proud that your creations are representing the whole of humanity in this, the first crewed space exploration outside our solar system."

Dr Roberts was uncharacteristically emotional. "Yes I am extremely proud of them all. I'd just like to point out that their involvement in the space mission was a result of direct discussions between ISA and the transapients. They are independent beings and it was they who decided to volunteer for this assignment."

Steve nodded his agreement. "That's right, Dr Roberts. I was very impressed by their capabilities – they even negotiated radical changes to the mission objectives. This was originally to have been a one way mission, but now these brave individuals will hopefully return to complete a round trip of some 8.5 light years."

The interviewer turned to Dr Roberts. "Dr Roberts, just what will the transapients currently be feeling as they embark on this historic mission?"

Dr Roberts looked at the couple walking through the entry tunnel to the waiting space jet. "Their minds are essentially human, inheriting their donor's characteristics and personality. They will be experiencing a range of emotions as any human would do in their position."

The whole world waited as last minute checks were undertaken. The minutes ticked by until eventually the space jet was cleared of surrounding structures and ready for take-off. This was somewhat less spectacular than the earlier vertical rocket launches of the Apollo and Space Shuttle era. A puff of dust from beneath the space jet signalled that the jet was now in motion. After a few seconds it soared into the sky and the crowds cheered as the jet veered away on a cushion of air. Alf#2 watched the ground recede behind them as the jet climbed higher. In a matter of minutes they were reaching the outer limits of the atmosphere, the lift provided by air flow was decreasing with altitude and the jet slowly split into two bodies; one optimised for spaceflight where Alf#2 and Louisa#2 sat, observing the smooth mechanics of spaceflight, the other larger body that had been a harness for the smaller craft, proceeding on its return trip to the launch pad.

The spacecraft accelerated towards a rendezvous orbit where it was to meet up with the antimatter fuelled spacecraft M2C that had arrived on schedule from the asteroid belt; the location of the antimatter production units. The spacecrafts slowly merged together and finally docked. The chamber that was now home to the transapients, moved silently from the conventional space vehicle to the antimatter spacecraft M2C.

A mining officer returning from a lengthy period working on the asteroid mining operation, made his way from M2C to the earthbound spacecraft. His trip would be a comfortable return journey that would meet up with the space jet and glide back down to earth; soon he would be reunited with his family. He did not envy the transapients with their immense journey ahead but he, like everyone else who had ever looked up at the stars in wonder, would be watching their progress with great interest.

The spacecrafts then slowly separated and the antimatter craft was left alone with nothing but 4.2 lightyears of empty space between it and its remote destination, Proxima-B.

Even though the launch of M2C would again be far less dramatic than the chemically powered rockets of the past, the media had succeeded in focusing billions of human minds on this, the official start of the journey. The transapients monitored the final automatic check sequences, while the world looked over their shoulder.

During their flight to rendezvous with M2C, Alf#2 and Louisa#2 had been kept busy unpacking their 'spare' transapient. The protective cover was removed to reveal the body of an inert transapient laying on her back as if asleep. Amelia#1 opened her eyes and looked up at the two smiling transapients. "Are we there yet?" she quipped.

Alf#2 laughed and helped her to her seat. "Not quite, but I'm afraid we are due for a live broadcast of the official voyage start to ten billion humans in about fifteen minutes."

"That should be interesting," smirked Amelia#1.

“Yes,” said Louisa#2 slowly. “I’m just wondering what some of those ten billion people will think of our transapient stowaway. Just remember that you are officially transapient spare parts.”

Alf#2 nodded in agreement. “That’s right. A complete set of spare parts including a mind of its own,” he noted.

Amelia#1 could not contain her excitement. “I’ll be on my bestest behaviour,” she announced.

The minutes passed by and the transapients tried to look sensible as they received the cue for their live broadcast.

## Chapter 37

# Double Trouble

The interview with Dr Roberts and Steve Bradshaw was interrupted by the imminent official start of the transapients journey. "Sorry to interrupt you Dr Roberts, but we are now going over for a live interview with the crew of the interstellar spacecraft M2C, where the transapients are preparing to embark on this historic voyage to our nearest neighbour star, Proxima Centauri."

An image of three smiling transapients appeared and the commentator was momentarily lost for words as he surveyed the unexpected scene. In his mind he was counting the faces; one, two… three? Two transapients had boarded the craft and yet there were now three faces smiling back at him. At first he thought it was an aberration in the video link, but then he saw that they were all moving independently. Yes there were Mr and Mrs Butler, he recognised straight away, but the third unexpected face looked strangely familiar. He looked at the face and then turned to ask Dr Roberts about the third crew member. "Dr Roberts, who …," his voice trailed off as he looked at Dr Roberts who sat looking slightly uncomfortable next to Steve, who was now also staring at Dr Roberts and then back to the remote image of Amelia#1.

The billions of hypernet viewers were now equally puzzled by the unfolding revelation. Gradually more and more viewers were enlarging the image of Amelia#1, and then enlarging the image of Dr Roberts, who had nowhere to hide. She coughed nervously as the whole world waited for an explanation. "Ladies and Gentlemen, I would like to introduce you to our spare crew member, Amelia."

Steve was the first to break the stunned silence. “When you said that there were spare parts, I did not realise it would comprise a complete transapient!” After a few moments in which the commentator was still trying to make sense of Dr Roberts’ ‘twin’ who had magically appeared on M2C, a sudden realisation dawned on Steve on top of the fact that Amelia was a transapient of Dr Roberts. “Wait a moment,” said Steve. “Who was at our first meeting? Was it you or Amelia?”

Dr Roberts smiled apologetically. “It was Amelia,” she admitted, “and yes she is a transapient of myself,” she added by way of explanation to the confused commentator. Steve reflected on the meeting several months earlier. No wonder he had been so impressed by Dr Roberts’ detailed knowledge of antimatter and space travel.

“Why did you keep the existence of this transapient quiet?” he asked. He was not annoyed; just curious.

“I wanted to see how my transapient would cope with an important encounter,” said Dr Roberts. It was true, but she did not want to admit to the world that in addition this transapient had not been approved by ABC-Tech. Dr James rolled his eyes as he watched the broadcast. Yet again Dr Roberts had ignored protocol and generated an unofficial transapient. But then he thought of the benefits of having two Dr Roberts to work with until he remembered that this transapient was about to disappear for 30 years on a space mission.

Finally the commentator regained his composure enough to turn to Steve. “Mr Bradshaw, does this ‘stowaway’ jeopardise the mission in any way?”

“Well, technically Amelia can be classed as a spare part, albeit a whole transapient. Her presence as a complete transapient has not changed the spacecraft’s dry mass, so there is no reason as far as I am concerned why the mission should not go ahead as planned.”

The world gave a collective sigh of relief. The countdown to launch could continue.

“You’re good to go,” announced the commentator. “We wish you good fortune on your mission, and we look forward to following your progress across the vast space to our nearest stellar neighbour.”

This launch was even less dramatic that the space jet lift off. When the time came to engage the gamma ray thruster all the transapients could hear was a faint hum. M2C was now being powered by antimatter annihilation. The mass was being converted into thruster energy with 40% efficiency, and M2C was soon accelerating at a constant 10 m/s every second. This had always been a popular acceleration as it provided an artificial gravity for the crew; they would feel the same weight for the first and last 4 months of the journey.

The commentator could barely contain his excitement. A minute had passed since M2C started. “How fast are they travelling now?” he asked.

“Nearly twice the speed of sound” said Steve. “They have only travelled 18 km.”

“That does not sound very far,” noted the commentator. “Is there something wrong?”

“No, no,” reassured Steve. “It takes some time to build up the speed; but remember this spacecraft is accelerating at 1g all the time for the first four months, unlike the earlier spacecraft which would cruise for much of their journeys without thrust, occasionally using gravitational sling shots around planets to increase speed. In just 26 minutes it will be travelling faster than the Voyager probes; that’s 16 kilometers every second.”

The commentator's eyes were glazing over – he could not comprehend these speeds. Sensing the intrigue surrounding the unexpected additional transapient, he decided to change the topic. "Dr Roberts, do you have anything to say to your transapients as they prepare to leave our solar system?"

Dr Roberts gazed at the three transapients smiling back at her. "You are heading off on an incredible journey; a journey that I have only dared dream of. That dream will be experienced by you my transapients and I am pleased that part of me will be there to explore the fascinating worlds so far away."

Amelia#1 knew how Dr Roberts would be feeling; proud of her achievements and the opportunity for them to fulfil their potential, carrying the hopes of humanity into space beyond the solar system. "Everything is great here," said Amelia#1. "All systems are operational, and all we need to do at the moment is sit back and enjoy the view." She felt a strong connection with the blue planet beneath them, knowing that billions of people would be watching their progress. After an hour the Earth was beginning to visibly shrink before them – this view from M2C was being beamed back to the billions of viewers reflecting on their home planet.

In two and a half hours M2C was just beyond the Moon's orbit and travelling at 86 kilometres every second. The Earth appeared to be Moon size, speed records for crewed flight were tumbling and M2C was still accelerating.

## Chapter 38

# Beyond the Solar System

After just 36 hours M2C was beyond the orbit of Mars. Early missions to Mars had taken months to make the trip. Alf#2 looked at the view towards Earth which had now shrunk to a star like object and the Sun was now 63% of its normal size as viewed from Earth.

In four days M2C was beyond the orbit of Jupiter and travelling at 3500 kilometres every second. After another two days Saturn's orbit had been reached and at the end of mission day ten the outer planet Neptune's orbit marked the extent of the solar system with respect to planets. M2C was now travelling at 10,000 kilometres every second or 3% of the speed of light. Within two weeks M2C was leaving the solar system and heading off on its lonely journey through interstellar space still accelerating at 1g.

At Neptune's distance radio waves would now take more than six hours to reach Earth, so interaction would be limited to bulk transfer of telemetry and video status reports. The Sun was now only 3% of its familiar size as viewed from Earth, while Proxima Centauri was still a single distant spec within the 100 billion stars of the Galaxy.

Amelia#1 surveyed their route on a three dimensional representation of the stars positions. The image showed the destination planet's parent star Proxima Centauri, a red dwarf star loosely bound to a binary star system 0.2 light years or 500 Neptune orbits away called Alpha Centauri; from Earth Alpha Centauri appeared as a bright single object in the constellation of Centaurus. Amelia#1 was able to get some idea of the cosmic scale by zooming out from this location. First of all neighbouring stars began to appear as the scale continued to change in factors of ten. Eventually the stars began to form a shape which would soon become recognizable as a spiral arm of the galaxy. After more zooming out the whole galaxy shrank to a fuzzy smear and eventually another galaxy, Andromeda appeared.

Alf#2 was watching this image with interest. “How far away is the Andromeda galaxy?” he asked.

“2.5 million light years,” replied Amelia#1. “We don’t have enough fuel to get there, but if we did and kept accelerating at 1g it would only take about 60 years to get there and back”.

“But isn’t our speed limited to the speed of light?” asked Alf#2.

“It is for someone observing the trip from Earth. It would take five million years for the trip, but the crew would only experience sixty years of travel.” Alf#2 still looked confused. “Moving clocks go very slow at speeds approaching that of light,” she added. “It’s a relativistic effect we don’t normally notice”.

“So will we have aged less than people on Earth when we return,” asked Alf#2 curiously.

“Yes, but only 18 months; we will be cruising at a third the speed of light and the time dilation is only 5 percent at this speed”.

Alf#2 nodded, but his lifetime of experience was at more sedate relative speeds where the time dilation was not noticeable; this made it difficult to conceive that the passage of time would be different between the static and travelling observers.

*

A very similar conversation was occurring between Amelia#2 and Alf#1 some 7.3 billion kilometres away back on Earth.

“I know it’s hard to believe,” said Amelia#1. “But just to prove it to ourselves, Amelia#2 and I have synchronized our body clocks so we will be able to actually measure the difference when she returns thirty years from now."

Alf#1 still looked incredulously at Amelia#1 and shook his head.

"Time is a mysterious quantity," sighed Dr Roberts as she examined the three dimensional rendition of the star positions that Amelia#2 was showing Alf#1. A small green tetrahedron represented the position of M2C which was barely beyond the outer solar system. "I will be seventy five when they return and yet you transapients will be practically unchanged; then you *will* look like my children," she laughed at the sudden realisation.

"And mine," said Louisa looking at Alf#1 and Louisa#1. The length of the space mission was highlighting the frailty of humans compared to transapients. "By the way Dr Roberts," she added, wanting to change the subject, "does anyone know about your second transapient, Amelia#2?"

"No, I have managed to keep her existence quiet for the time being," admitted Dr Roberts.

"Unlike Amelia#1!" said Amelia#2. "Her existence was broadcast to the whole planet while you were being interviewed!"

"Yes, that was quite an embarrassing moment," said Dr Roberts grimacing at the memory. "But I think that the publicity for transapients has definitely taken an upturn now; people are realising some of their remarkable capabilities."

"And no one has been asking about our identities recently? We're still disguised as Louisa's mysterious sister and husband," said Louisa.

"No they haven't," said Dr Roberts. "But I think we should keep a low profile for the time being. I will continue to work at ABC-Tech, where I can field any questions about transapients without drawing attention to you all."

## Chapter 39

# Time to Leave

In the following weeks the publicity and interest surrounding the progress of the spacecraft M2C remained intense. Everyone had their own three dimensional model of the route being taken by the transapients showing their position and speed. M2C would continue accelerating for another fourteen weeks until it reached one third light speed.

The duration of the mission was playing on Louisa's mind. It had made her think about the future of both herself and the transapients. At the moment Alf#1 was just like Alf – he could not be more like Alf. But he was an Alf who had effectively stopped aging. They would not grow old together as normal human couples. And then there was Louisa#1. For her it would be the same; impervious to the relentless march of time. Louisa had always intended that Louisa#1 would one day be a soul partner for Alf#1. They were compatible; they had shared memories and experiences of Louisa and Alf's life together. Perhaps it was time to leave the transapients to their future now, rather than later as she had originally intended.

It was the hardest decision of her life, but Louisa gradually became more certain that this was what she wanted to do. It would be difficult to leave her husband, but she would still be with him in the form of Louisa#1 and she would be able to watch both transapient couples from afar. She would become a spectator of her own dual transapient lives.

She left a message with Amelia#2 for Dr Roberts explaining her decision and suggesting that Louisa#1 should adopt Louisa's identity; the fictitious sister of Louisa. To begin with Dr Roberts was shocked at Louisa's departure. She had imagined her and Alf#1 staying together, but after a while she understood that this was another selfless act from Louisa.

Louisa#1 was transformed into Louisa's 'sister' at ABC-Tech. Alf#1 felt very sad that Louisa had gone. He would have looked after Louisa for the rest of her days. Louisa#1 knew how Louisa had come to her decision and had mixed feelings. She was an extension of Louisa's life so she hoped that Alf#1 would come to regard her as the same person.

A month had passed since M2C had been launched. The three dimensional route model showed their position as ten times the orbit of Neptune, and travelling at twenty five thousand kilometres every second or ten percent the speed of light. Messages would now take 30 hours to reach Earth from M2C or vice versa. Alf#1 and Louisa#1 sent a video message to Alf#2 and Louisa#2 to explain why Louisa#1 now looked like Louisa. The news of Louisa's departure was received 30 billion kilometres away with a mixture of surprise and sadness.

"She's doing it for Alf#1," said Louisa#2 turning away from the video message. "She is giving Louisa#1 her identity so that she will become a transapient couple with Alf#1."

Alf#2 was still trying to understand why she would leave her husband. Amelia#1 knew that Louisa had specifically asked Dr Roberts to create a second transapient of herself ultimately as a partner for Alf#1. She looked at Louisa#2. "You are a very considerate person," she whispered.

*

The weeks sped by and on Christmas day 2060 at a distance of over 500 billion kilometres the thruster on M2C was turned off and the crew were now weightless without the constant acceleration that had propelled them to the current velocity. The spacecraft would coast at this speed for the next thirteen years. The remaining antimatter fuel would be preserved for slowing down as the spacecraft neared its destination, and then for the return trip. Messages were now taking twenty days to traverse the widening gap between M2C and Earth. The transapients had anticipated this delay and sent Christmas greetings to each other in advance, so that they would arrive on the correct day. Jamie had sent a message to Alf#2 pointing out that he would be twice his current age when M2C arrived at Proxima B.

The Sun had become just another star in the blackness of space, albeit much brighter than any of the other visible stars. M2C was now travelling at one third the speed of light. Forward looking sensors deployed each side of the spacecraft were probing the path ahead, on the lookout for any objects that might damage the spacecraft at this speed. The previous miniature robotic mission had just relied on a large number of small spacecraft to achieve its goal; the loss of a few small spacecraft from collisions could be tolerated. This was not the case for M2C; it did not have this redundancy. Even small particles of interstellar dust could inflict significant damage at this speed. Tiny course corrections would be made to avoid any large impact. A self-regenerating deflection shield in front of the spacecraft was designed to minimise damage for any smaller particles which should impact the spacecraft.

The transapient's nanobots were kept busy repairing molecular damage caused by cosmic radiation. The brain connections and memory storage had built in redundancy and background routines which would detect damage and initiate repairs. This redundancy meant that there would be no long term loss of data or functionality.

They decided that they would shut down for most of the trip with monthly active days to check that M2C was in a healthy state and send back regular status reports via the laser communications link aimed precisely at the distant Earth. Each report would show that the spacecraft had travelled another 60 solar system radii.

“Fancy a game of Chess?” ventured Alf#2, when Amelia#1 had finished her monthly progress report.

“I thought you’d never ask,” beamed Amelia#1.

There were no physical chess pieces – the virtual game was shared between the two transapients who each set about analysing millions of potential moves. Alf#2 knew he would not stand much chance against Amelia#2’s natural flare for the game, but he enjoyed the challenge. And after all – they had all the time in the world.

# Chapter 40

# The Long Coast

The months rolled by as M2C coasted onwards towards Proxima Centauri. With the expanding distance from Earth, each monthly report was taking an extra ten days to propagate the vast distance compared to the previous monthly report. After 6 months the time between reports the laser signal would take eighty days to reach Earth, so the June's progress report would not be received until September.

The reduction in reporting frequency mirrored the gradual reduction in media coverage. With no sensational news to report interest in the mission had been put on hold, with another thirteen years of coasting to go.

Another activity put on hold back on Earth was the creation of any more transapients. Dr Roberts' unofficial creation of her own transapient (Amelia#1) had not gone down well with ABC-Tech. She had not been dismissed; her services were needed as a key consultant for the inter-stellar mission. Dr James had been given strict instructions to ensure that there were no more irregular activities at ABC-Tech by working closely with Dr Roberts at all times.

Meanwhile on M2C, Amelia#1 was conducting a routine health diagnostic on the spacecraft's dormant antimatter drive system. This was the first major flight for an antimatter driven spacecraft and the potential energy stored in the several thousand kilogram of antimatter required critical design to ensure isolation. Amelia#1 stared at the field isolator subsystem telemetry; there was an anomaly in the measured field strength; it was significantly lower than nominal and the antimatter fuel was already displaced a few microns from its normal position. Amelia#1 quickly accessed the archived readings; this confirmed that the field strength had been dropping for the last three days. At this rate the isolation unit would fail within the next twenty four hours; the result would be the largest man-made explosion in human history as two thousand kilogram of antimatter would be instantly annihilated, releasing the equivalent to the detonation of forty three thousand megatons of explosives, seven times the yield of the entire nuclear stockpile at the beginning of the century.

"Er…, not quite sure how to break this to you guys," said Amelia#1 quietly. "We have a major problem," She quickly explained the impending failure of the antimatter containment field and the catastrophic consequences. They were all aware of the spacecraft's design and operation. There was only one option for this eventuality; the antimatter core needed to be jettisoned to isolate it from the spacecraft's matter and hence – prevent the otherwise inevitable annihilation. "We need to start the process as soon as possible," she concluded urgently.

Three hours later, the transapients watched with relief as the antimatter core separated from the spacecraft. Louisa#2 gazed at the spherical container that housed the antimatter. "Without the antimatter, how are we going to slow down?" she asked, but she already knew the answer.

"I'm afraid we can't," said Amelia#1. They were on a spacecraft with no brakes, hurtling towards Proxima Centauri, with only a small amount of conventional propellant for course corrections and planetary exploration; this would provide nothing compared to the energy needed to slow down the spacecraft its current one third light speed. "I've sent an emergency report back to Earth, but it will take eighty days to get there and by then we will be another twenty seven light days from Earth. And then their reply will take more than one hundred and twenty days to reach us."

Alf#2 and Louisa#2 contemplated their situation. The mission would now be a rapid fly-by without much more information to gather than the previous miniature space probes had reported the previous year. They were on a one way trip to the end of the universe. Amelia#1 could not help thinking about Newton's first law of motion; *an object in motion continues in motion with the same speed and in the same direction unless acted upon by an unbalanced force.* How could they possibly find the force they needed; tantalizingly the energy source that would do the job was now floating only a few kilometres from M2C.

*

Steve Bradshaw sat at his desk reflecting on the mission he had organised. After the seemingly non-stop whirlwind of attention the mission had received at its launch, he now felt that he actually had time to relax and live life at a more tolerable pace. He stretched his arms high above his head releasing the tension that had built up over the last few months.

He froze in mid-stretch as an unscheduled message appeared in front of him from M2C:

*Regret to report that there has been a failure of the antimatter containment field generator.*
*Antimatter core has been ejected. You may want to modify the mission objectives.*

He read the short message several times. The concise report left little doubt to its meaning, but he was finding it hard to take in. The antimatter containment design had been the hardest part of the mission; how to control so much potential energy. It was a design that could not easily be tested; of course simulations had been made and small scale models had been tested, but there would always be a finite probability of failure on the spacecraft version.

“Dr Roberts, we need a meeting urgently!” said Steve when he finally contacted Dr Roberts. He was trying to keep his voice under control. “We have a major problem with M2C.” He had found solutions for many technical problems in the past, but this one seemed literally beyond his reach.

## Chapter 41

# Help!

Dr Roberts sent Amelia#2 to the meeting. Amelia#2 was best equipped to assist with any technical problems – she had a working knowledge of M2C's design as she had received matrix updates of Amelia#1 prior to the launch of M2C.

"Good evening Dr Roberts," said Steve. "Thank you for meeting me at such short notice." Steve explained M2C's problem briefly and Amelia#2 immediately began to analyse possible solutions.

"How long would it take to prepare the back up space vehicle for a rescue mission?" asked Amelia#2.

"Well, if we pulled out all the stops we could be ready in two months," said Steve slowly.

"And could we take a spare antimatter isolator?" asked Amelia#2.

"That should be possible too. What are you proposing Dr Roberts?" asked Steve in wonder.

"If we accelerate for two extra weeks compared to M2C we can catch up and rendezvous with M2C in a rescue spacecraft in 7 years, leaving plenty of time to rescue the transapients and even complete the mission."

Steve felt like he had been in this position before when he had eventually found out that in retrospect he had been talking to a transapient. "Dr Roberts, are you human?" he asked her directly. Amelia#2 shook her head. Steve was not totally surprised. He knew that Dr Roberts had previously created unofficial transapients – so he guessed this was probably another.

"So does this mean you are willing to crew the rescue spacecraft?" Steve asked.

"Yes. Along with two others," added Amelia#2. "Our crew will comprise exactly the same set of transapients as that on M2C," she concluded.

"I see." Steve was not sure whether he was shocked or relieved by the swiftness of the solution presented to him. "Well, if we are going to launch within two months we had better start making arrangements immediately. I trust you will gather your other crew members."

"I will brief them immediately," said Amelia#2. In her mind she was doing cartwheels in anticipation of joining the other transapients on their space mission.

"And I will send M2C a message," said Steve. "Although it will take 143 days to get to them, by which time hopefully you should be travelling at one quarter light speed and still accelerating."

The following two months were spent preparing the rescue spacecraft which became known as M2C2 along with a containment field generator. The transapients were already familiar with the spacecraft operation so the crew were prepared long before the anticipated launch date. The M2C crisis had rekindled intense interest in the mission now that there was also a rescue element to be reported. Eyebrows were raised once more when it became known that a second transapient version of Dr Roberts would be part of the crew.

M2C2 was ready for launch a few days later than planned. Extra effort had been taken to improve the reliability of the containment field generator. As M2C2 started its acceleration with all three transapients on board, it was hard to believe that the spacecraft would eventually catch up with M2C in seven years' time. Dr Roberts was feeling anxious now that all her creations were speeding out of the solar system with uncertain futures. She had invested so much time and care into their creation; she had mixed feelings about the situation. Amelia#2, on the other hand, was eager to embark in this immense pursuit of M2C "Let's go!" she yelled as the 1g of acceleration kicked in. Alf#1 and Louisa#1 smiled at Amelia#2's enthusiasm. They were keen to rescue the other transapients but not quite so keen on the details of how this would be achieved.

*

Meanwhile on M2C, Alf#2 wanted to know if there was any prospect at all of regaining control of their spacecraft. Amelia#1 was not about to offer false hope. "We do not have the material or processes to repair the containment field generator. I think we should await a response from Earth in case they have any ideas. If they responded immediately to our report, we should get a response in 83 days. The finite speed of light becomes quite a nuisance at these distances."

*

83 days later and M2C had travelled another 27 light days and M2C2 had reached one quarter light speed. The message that had been sent two months earlier was nearing its destination. The suspense on M2C was increasing as each transapient wondered whether Mission Control had a solution, or that they were destined to continue across the galaxy at their current unstoppable speed; *to infinity and beyond* as Amelia#1 had joked.

"We've just received a message," announced Amelia#1. Alf#2 and Louisa#2 took a few nanoseconds to interpret the message:

*DON'T PANIC!*
*M2C2 and transapient rescue crew on their way. Rendezvous in 7 years.*
*See you later*

The first line of the message made Amelia#1 laugh. The fitting catchphrase quote from *The Hitchhiker's Guide to the Galaxy* had not been lost on her. "Looks like we will be expecting company in seven years' time," said Amelia#1.

"That's amazing," said Alf#2. "How did they manage to arrange a rescue mission so quickly?"

"I was hoping that they would have a spare flight model," said Amelia#1. "But even so, I am impressed with their rapid response."

"I get the feeling that Amelia#2 may have had something to do with it," said Louisa#2. "I was about to have transapient kittens."

Hope had returned to the crew of M2C. It did not worry the transapients that it would be another seven years before M2C2 would catch up with them – time was not a problem for them.

## Chapter 42

# Cruise Control

M2C2 continued accelerating for another 50 days. The thruster was then disabled and M2C2 began its long cruise at a constant speed 16% faster than M2C. The distance between the two spacecrafts was now reducing by 15,000 kilometres every second.

Millions of viewers on Earth and the two sets of transapients had updated their three dimensional models to include both spacecraft positions. Two small green tetrahedrons now represented the position of M2C and M2C2.

Dr Roberts and Steve Bradshaw gathered around their model. "Well, we now have a long wait, but not as long as the trip to Proxima Centauri," said Steve. "They will be two light years away when they meet up for their high speed rescue. They will effectively be on their own. We will not know the result of that rescue for two years after the event."

"They'll cope with the challenge," said Dr Roberts. "They are remarkably innovative and with six of them working together, I think they will be able to solve most problems that might come their way."

"I hope so," said Steve. "I still can't get used to how quickly they can digest information."

"Yes, they have remarkable capacity to analyse problems coupled with human judgement," said Dr Roberts.

"And there are no more versions Dr Roberts left on Earth that I am not aware of?" asked Steve.

"No, there are no transapients on Earth. I am strictly forbidden to make any more at the moment. ABC-Tech considers that six transapients is plenty at this stage of their introduction. Maybe things will change when they return."

"By the way," said Steve, "I sent a message to both spacecrafts containing the design updates that have been made to the containment field generator, and procedures for recovering the ejected antimatter core. The message will take 25 days to get to M2C2 and a further 16 weeks to get to M2C. If this works out we could have two spacecraft arriving at Proxima Centauri in 14 years' time."

*

The months rolled by and once again the media frenzy surrounding the project subsided after a surge in interest when the news broke about a rescue mission. When Mrs Jones heard the news, she was pleased that more transapients had been removed from Earth and secretly hoped that the mission would end in disaster. She was, however, in the minority. Jamie's interest in the mission never waned; he was now in contact with both Dr Roberts and Steve Bradshaw; asking detailed questions about the mission.

After four years into the mission the gap between M2C and M2C2 was down to 70 light days and M2C was now one light year from Earth. Jamie was now studying Advanced Maths and Applied Physics and was set to join ISA for a career in space exploration. He was already studying the telemetry data received by both spacecraft and exchanging messages with both Alf#1 and Alf#2 on each spacecraft.

Another three years passed, Jamie had graduated and was now at ISA's ground control working directly with Steve Bradshaw. It was August 27$^{th}$ 2067 and time for M2C2 to engage reverse thruster which would slow down the spacecraft to M2C's speed in 16 days.

The transapients in M2C2 experienced the deceleration of 1g while the spacecraft slowed. Eventually the spacecrafts' trajectories merged and their separation slowly reduced as M2C2's thruster was turned off; both spacecraft were now hurtling along at one third light speed.

Amelia#1 greeted their space colleagues "Glad you could join us," she said; at last they could talk interactively without the inconvenience of significant radio propagation delays.

"Hello everyone, we were just passing and heard that you might need a tow to the nearest star system," said Amelia#2 jovially.

"Yes please, but it's more that we need to have our brakes looked at," said Amelia#1.

"Well you are in luck there," said Amelia#2. "We happen to have bought some spares with us, so hopefully we'll be able to make you space worthy again before you know it."

"Much obliged," said Amelia#1. This was echoed by cheers from Alf#2 and Louisa#2.

The next two days were spent preparing for the sensitive operation of retrieving the antimatter core which had been parked on a parallel trajectory a few kilometres away. Alf#1 made his way to the exit hatch and slowly opened the door to the empty space beyond. He did not have a bulky spacesuit to impede him, just a thruster pack to allow spacewalk manoeuvre, and the replacement field generator unit buckled to his arm. As he drifted slowly towards the antimatter core he felt the enormity of space around him. With no spacecraft shell there was nothing between him and the surrounding patchwork of stars that made up the galactic backdrop.

A short squirt of reverse thrust was enough to bring him to a halt in front of the sphere of antimatter. If he touched the antimatter the energy released would be unimaginable; both spacecrafts and their watching occupants would be destroyed in an instant.

Two matching hemispherical cups were positioned either side of the ball of antimatter, each with its own field generator designed to keep the antimatter suspended within a shell. Millimetre by millimetre the cups moved over the antimatter ball until they encompassed the ball and locked together to form a spherical shell.

Alf#1 checked the position of the antimatter and raised a thumb towards the two spacecraft. M2C's energy source was back under control. The transapients heaved a collective sigh of relief whereas Steve, Dr Roberts and Jamie back on Earth could only stare at the time and hope that the procedure was successful.

The antimatter core was now ready to make its way back to M2C, a relatively simple manoeuvre. The following day was spent running through checks that the core was fully integrated back into the heart of M2C's thruster system. "We've got our brakes back; the mission can continue as planned," announced Amelia#1. "We even have a spare spacecraft now." She immediately sent a status report to Earth with the news of the rescue mission, but it would take two years to reach its destination, and by that time they would be one light year from Proxima Centauri.

## Chapter 43

# Contact

As the months rolled on further, the transapients settled into their routines, relieved that disaster had been averted; they would not now be condemned to an eternal inter galactic journey. As they reached the final light year of their journey the message which had been sent two years previously arrived at Earth. Jamie punched the air in celebration as he took in the news. He was now a leading consultant on the mission, and was responsible for disseminating the news to the wider world. Mrs Jones rolled her eyes as she could not help noticing the news of the rescue mission. She would never accept transapients as fellow beings, and was intimidated by their continued success and the public adulation of their achievements.

Meanwhile Amelia#1 had been studying the distant Proxima Centauri, scanning the region in every possible electro-magnetic wavelength. Then she stopped at a particular band and adjusted the sensitivity with a highly directional receiver to reduce the background noise. She could just detect a faint repetitive signal among the background noise. She contacted Amelia#2. "Hello Amelia," she said. "I seem to be picking up a periodic signal from the direction of Proxima Centauri."

"That's a coincidence," said Amelia#1. "I was just about to call you with the same observation."

"We should be able to get a fix and enhance reception using our combined readings," said Amelia#2. A few moments later they had determined that the source was consistent with the position of Proxima B and then simultaneously they recognised the repeating pattern that was being transmitted; the first twelve prime numbers up to 31. The number 2, 3, 5, 7, 11, 13, 15, 17, 19, 23, 29 and 31 were being repeated over and over.

“What does it mean?” asked Louisa#2. “It looks like some kind of beacon.”

“It is a beacon,” stated Amelia#1. “It is announcing intelligence using an irregular pattern, so it is not confused with natural pulsar emissions. It is using the universal truth of mathematics; the building blocks of number theory; prime numbers. Think of it as a *Hello World* message.”

“Of course,” said Alf#2. He had been teaching maths for years but never thought of it as a basis as a universally recognizable language. Of course numbers could be used to represent language – but how would you communicate with an alien lifeform without some common understanding? Universally understood, a sequence of primes were the natural choice to announce ‘I am an intelligent lifeform’. The irregular sequence of primes would make them easily distinguishable from naturally occurring transmissions such as pulsars.

“Oh my goodness,” said Louisa#2. “We have probably just witnessed the first contact with an alien lifeform. What do we do now?”

Amelia#1 had already considered this eventuality. “They are likely to be more advanced than us. Humans have only been using electromagnetic transmissions for the last 170 years. On a cosmic timescale this is a microscopic duration. We should announce our understanding and intelligence by sending a repetition of the next seven prime numbers.”

“Why seven?” asked Louisa#2.

"They are using binary groupings; they are transmitting the first set of prime numbers less than 32," said Amelia#1. "The natural extension is the next set of prime numbers up to 64. We should repeatedly transmit the numbers 37, 41, 43, 47, 53, 59 and 61, as an acknowledgement of their transmission on a harmonic frequency. It will take a year for the signal to get to Proxima Centauri, but it will give us some time to establish a dialogue. As this is a historic decision, are we all agreed on this course of action?"

All transapients registered their agreement. There was no time to ask mission control back on Earth. It would now take three years to send a message and four years to receive a response and they were only three years away from Proxima Centauri. They sent a report back to Earth to advise mission control of the historic event.

Eighteen months later the transapients were six light months from Proxima Centauri. Both spacecraft waited expectantly, monitoring the repetitive prime sequence that had not changed since they first picked up the curious signal. The signal had increased in intensity by virtue of the reduced range but was otherwise identical in its format.

Then it happened, just as Amelia was going over and over the sequence comprising 37, 41, 43, 47, 53, 59 and 61 that was being transmitted to Proxima Centauri, the received sequence changed to 67, 71, 73, 79, 83 and 89; the next six prime numbers between 64 and 96.

"Now we know that they know we are intelligent," said Amelia#1.

"And we know that they know we know they are intelligent," said Amelia#2.

"Stop it you two," said Alf#1. "Do we send the next sequence?" he asked.

"Yes," said Amelia#2. "We will repeatedly send the next set; 97, 101, 103, 107, 109, 113 and 127. They should have a good idea how far away we are now and how fast we are moving towards them. We should get something back in three months' time."

Three months later a signal was received, but it was not a set of prime numbers. Alf#2 looked at the millions of numbers being received. "They appear to be grouped into sets of three numbers. The first and second numbers are evenly spread across two 20 bit values, whereas the third number is a 32 bit value with a much smaller spread."

Alf#1 immediately recognized what these numbers could be. "They are co-ordinates for some kind of heat map," he said.

"A heat map?" said Louisa#1. "Are they trying to send us instructions?"

"Let's see," said Amelia#2. "What would be the simplest three dimensional co-ordinate system?"

"Polar co-ordinates I would think," said Alf#2. "That would make the first two numbers latitude and longitude, yes the first two numbers might represent the co-ordinates on a sphere."

"And the third number," said Amelia#1 "could be a value associated with that co-ordinate".

"A digital elevation map of height above the planet's surface?" suggested Amelia#2. "Let's feed the numbers into our three dimensional model scaled to Proxima-B."

A few moments later a three dimensional rendition of Proxima B floated in front of each transapient trio. They all recognized the image, it was a rotated version of the image beamed back to Earth from the miniature space probes eight years earlier. Amelia adjusted the orientation of the image to match their familiar view of Proxima B which had caused quite a stir when it was first received at Earth.

“How should we respond to this message now we know what it means?” asked Alf#1.

“Well I suggest we send an elevation map of Earth in the same format,” said Amelia#1. “That will show we understand the message and show them where we come from.”

A few moments later Amelia#1 had converted an elevation map of Earth to the same format as that used to represent Proxima B, and initiated the transmission. A response was expected just before the reverse thrusters would be engaged for the last sixteen weeks of the journey.

# Chapter 44

# Star Date

As anticipated, a new message arrived five months before they were due to arrive at Proxima Centauri.

"It's changed and it's a smaller data set," said Amelia#1. "It seems to be in the same co-ordinate system, so I'll just feed the data into our model."

As the data streamed its way into the three dimensional model, the transapients watched as a trajectory emerged before them clearly intended as guidance for the spacecraft to enter a circular polar orbit around Proxima B.

"I think we must show good faith and follow the trajectory," said Amelia#2. The other transapients agreed. A new message was sent out relaying back the same trajectory as confirmation of reception and compliance to the implicit directive.

A few weeks later both spacecrafts engaged reverse thrust to begin the sixteen weeks it would take to slow down to a speed that would put them into an orbit around Proxima B. The polar orbit would be aligned with the curious ring that had been observed from the earlier mission images; the transition zone between the perpetual night/day boundary of the tidally locked planet. As the spacecrafts slowed at 1g the trajectory received in the data set was tweaked to reflect more accurate measurements that were being made remotely.

*

Jamie stared at his three dimensional model tracking the position of the two spacecraft and awaited any telemetry reports. They should now be approaching Proxima B. Only a few more weeks of deceleration and they would be there. However it would take four light years for any news of that event. Any reports coming in now would be from when the spacecraft was three light years away.

Then an unscheduled report was received. Jamie was the first person to digest the message.

“I don’t believe it!” he shouted.

Steve strolled over to Jamie to look over his shoulder “Don’t believe what?” asked Steve.

“Unless this is a transapient trick, they have just received an intelligent signal from Proxima B,” said Jamie staring up at Steve.

“It’s no trick,” said Steve. “Look, they have sent a sample of the received signal.”

“This is amazing,” said Jamie. “They have responded to the prime sequence signal. Well that has saved a lot of debate on Earth.”

“Yes. When this is announced there may be some nervous reaction to the news,” said Steve. “We should contact Dr Roberts first.”

Dr Roberts made her way straight from ABC-Tech to ISA control centre. “This must be important if it cannot be discussed on the hypernet,” she said as she arrived.

“We’ve had an unscheduled report from M2C,” said Steve.

“Is there a problem?” asked Dr Roberts.

“Not immediately – but something has happened which will affect both the mission and everyone on Earth.”

Jamie showed Dr Roberts the message. It took a few moments for the implications of the report to sink in. She put her hand to her mouth, her expression a mixture of shock and surprise. Eventually she composed herself enough to talk rationally again. “Does anyone else know about this yet?” she asked. Steve and Jamie shook their heads. “There are many people who believe we should not make contact with alien civilisations.”

“They have already responded,” said Jamie. “It is too late to stop it now. We gave the transapients independence and we knew they would face many challenges by themselves. We should trust their judgement.”

“I trust their judgement,” said Dr Roberts, “but I am not sure everyone else will.”

“Making contact with aliens carries risk,” said Steve. “But if we did not take risks, we would never explore beyond our back yard. I think we should release this to the media immediately. There is no point in supressing it further.”

Jamie made the announcement to the media a few hours later. The profound news gradually sank in and the questions started pouring in thick and fast. Did the transapients seek permission to respond to the alien signal? Should we abandon the mission? How long would it be before they paid us a visit?

Many of the hysterical questions came from reporters who had either forgotten or were ignorant of the large delays involved in corresponding with the transapients. It took a while to explain that right now the transapients had arrived at Proxima B and could well be getting to know their alien hosts. The exchange which was being monitored worldwide brought everyone up to date as much as the speed of light permitted. Mrs Jones shook her head. “I knew they were trouble,” she congratulated herself. She was one of the many who were apprehensive about the news; her satisfied smile soon turned to a worried frown. Even though they were four light years away, the transapients were still worrying Mrs Jones.

## Chapter 45

# A Close Encounter

The world's worries about alien interaction seemed a million miles away; in fact they were twenty five million million miles away. M2C and M2C2 were flying in close formation, following the mysterious third party prescribed trajectory; a circular polar orbit around Proxima B. The crew of each spacecraft watched the strange world beneath them bathed in the red light of its red dwarf parent star, Proxima Centauri. They were orbiting above the day/night transition; with the planet tidally locked to Proxima Centauri the rotation period matched the Proxima B eleven day 'year'; the same parched face was permanently pointing towards the red dwarf, while the cold dark side would face perpetual darkness.

They gazed at the thin strip near the day/night transition where Proxima Centauri would appear to always be hugging the horizon. It was here that any life would tend to develop, providing the least extreme conditions, and sure enough a green ring was evident near the transition point before it became shrouded in everlasting darkness.

It was a strange world; being slightly larger than the Earth it had enough gravitational pull to keep hold of its turbulent atmosphere. The static orientation of the planet's alignment with Proxima Centauri meant that the sub stellar point was always subject to the most intense radiation. The colder atmosphere from the dark side was constantly being drawn symmetrically towards this region and now the transapients had time to observe the atmospheric flows they could see that there was a constant bidirectional flow of low altitude cold gas flowing towards the daylight hemisphere and high altitude warm gas flowing outwards towards the shaded hemisphere. Where the two layers passed each other there were swirls of mixed gas which varied in density to produce what looked like smoke rings emanating from the sub stellar point.

After a while their quiet observation of the exoplanet was interrupted by Amelia#1. "I'm picking up some movement on the horizon," she announced. The spacecraft's sensors overlaid the object on their field of vision. It was rising slowly from the transition region, a large winged craft with a projected intercept point due in twenty minutes; it was an alien craft on its way to investigate the new arrivals.

The transapients inherited emotions of excitement mixed with apprehension were being experienced as the craft drew closer. Hopefully they had exhibited enough intelligence to be considered an interesting lifeform, and that they were not in any way a threat. They were all aware that this was a critical meeting which would need careful communication. "How do you say hello to an alien?" asked Louisa#2 nervously.

"I suggest we bow together," said Amelia#1. "There is no point saying too much when we do not have a common language."

The alien craft had come to a halt relative to M2C and M2C2 and an inviting hole had appeared in its side. Clearly the transapients were being asked to make the small step from their familiar craft to the unknown environment of the alien craft. "Should we all go?" asked Alf#2.

"I think we should keep together," said Amelia#2. "We are just going to have to trust our hosts and show willing."

One by one, the transapients made their way from M2C and M2C2 to the alien craft. They gathered inside the entrance area; they had not been together like this for seven years, but it was the wrong time for a reunion celebration. The hole that had opened up moments before now resealed itself behind them. The transapients were in the belly of the alien craft, and they sensed that they were on the move. But where they would be taken was a complete mystery.

Eventually the craft came to a stop and the hole in the side of the craft opened again. A deafening roar of wind greeted them as they stepped out into what appeared to be an enormous cave. A harsh cold wind was whistling past the cave entrance. Further into the cave was a smaller tunnel which looked far more inviting than the stormy winds outside. The transapients gravitated towards the tunnel using their infrared sensors. After several hundred metres the tunnel opened up into a large underground cavern. At the entrance to the cavern stood two figures; they turned towards the transapients as they approached, each had a pair of large round sensors which enabled them to determine the distance of any objects emitting a wide spectrum of electromagnetic wavelengths. The sensors which looked like large round eyes surveyed the transapients as they stopped in their tracks. Each transapient was then suddenly aware of a modulated radio transmission – the beings were using radio frequencies to communicate, but the data being transferred was not intelligible.

Amelia#1 made the first proactive move by sending the second set of seven prime numbers using the radio frequency that the aliens had just been using. She bowed slowly, as did the other transapients in unison; hopefully this transmission would be recognised and they would be acknowledged as intelligent beings.

A brief exchange of radio communication between the two aliens followed and then one of the aliens transmitted the third set of prime numbers and they both bowed together. Amelia#1 felt that although it would be difficult to communicate, it appeared that both parties were trying to establish common understanding; they should build on this initial exchange.

They had already successfully used graphical representation of the planet's topography and a spacecraft trajectory as a method of exchanging three dimensional images and an implicit directive. They had radio communication as a medium for exchanging information.

Amelia#1 then began to wonder how a lifeform would evolve radio as a method of communication; unless this was another evolutionary path that did not involve natural selection. Were these aliens the remnants of an advanced civilisation, just as transapients had been developed from humans? It was an interesting possibility but she was not yet equipped to find out the answer.

The two aliens floated across the ground a few metres and then turned to the transapients. "I think they want us to follow," said Louisa#1. When the aliens saw that the transapients were following slowly behind, they continued across the cavern to a waiting capsule.

"Looks like we are going on a city tour," said Alf#2. The capsule drifted silently across the cavern and into another tunnel where it gathered speed for a few minutes before eventually slowing to a stop in a maze of structures containing hundreds of aliens. It reminded Alf#2 of a beehive.

The two aliens floated out of the capsule and they all entered a small room where another alien stood as though deep in thought.

"I've been expecting you," he announced. The transapients could not believe what they were hearing.

# Chapter 46

# The Proximapients

“What’s going on?” asked Amelia#1 when she had got over the shock of a human voice in this alien environment.

“Forgive me,” said the alien. “Allow me to introduce myself. My name is Shpiliger#39872. Welcome to what you have named Proxima B.”

Ameila#1 had a hundred questions to ask all at once. She composed herself and rather than fire off her questions, decided the diplomatic course of action was to introduce themselves. “Thank you for your welcome,” she said. “I am Amelia#1 and this is Amelia#2, Alf#1, Louisa#1, Alf#2 and Louisa#2. We come from planet Earth over four light years from here.”

“We are impressed by your rapid progress,” said Shpiliger#39872. “We have been monitoring your transmissions from Earth for many of your Earth years. You have had a turbulent history, but you appear to be on the verge of exploring beyond your solar system. We noticed your fly by probes and we were on the lookout for a follow on mission.”

“How did you learn our language?” asked Louisa#2.

“Well we studied your transmissions and gradually built up an understanding. Many of us worked on deciphering your speech, but with a combination of language experts, huge volumes of radio transmissions, and a lot of time we have achieved an understanding; I can speak your language fluently.”

"Amazing," said Alf#2. "We thought there would be a language barrier."

"Have you visited our planet yet?" asked Amelia#2 curiously.

"No. We decided that your civilisation was not advanced enough to deal with extra-terrestrials; so we have been waiting for your technology to mature. In the last couple of hundred Earth years there has been quite a remarkable advancement in your capabilities. We knew you were on your way some time ago."

"Well, as you probably know," said Amelia#2 "we represent a new being derived from humans. We have many human traits but we are based on quite a different body composition."

"Indeed," said Shpiliger#39872 "we have had a similar development. Let me outline our history."

"That would be very interesting to hear," said Amelia#1.

"Well," said Shpiliger#39872 "our planet was once very similar to yours. It was spinning slowly and so we had equal night and day. Conditions were ideal for the development of life, apart from the occasional high energy flares that are typical of red dwarfs. Our red dwarf star gives out a lot less energy than your sun, so the region where life could develop was very close to the parent star. Life did develop but it was often nearly wiped out by high energy flares from Proxima B. Being so close to our parent star meant that tidal forces caused the planet spin rate slow until it eventually became tidally locked to Proxima Centauri. The advantage to this was that the perpetual dark side provided shelter from the flares. But life was still very susceptible living on the twilight zone which offered the most benign environmental conditions. During one particularly long flare free period the civilisation became advanced enough to develop intelligent beings based on themselves; sentient beings with intelligence and durability."

"And you are the result of that evolution," concluded Amelia#1.

"Yes, we are," said Shpiliger#39872. "We started our existence in these underground cities where our creators and ancestors could survive the occasional flares from Proxima Centauri."

"And where are your creators now," asked Amelia#2, intrigued by this parallel development.

"They died out many centuries ago. The planet was not stable and it could not sustain their population. We are both their legacy and their spirit that lives on in each of us. I am the 39,872$^{nd}$ Proximapient created from our ancestor Shpiliger.

"So we are not unique," Amelia#1 reflected. "It appears to be a normal evolutionary path to suddenly switch from natural selection to self-design. We have become our own creators."

"Yes, we have the ability to create more versions of ourselves," said Shpiliger#39872. We have extended the underground cities and advanced our technological capabilities to sustain our existence."

"We are the very first of our kind from Earth so we are an emergent being on our planet," said Amelia#2. "Our durability was the reason we were selected for the first interstellar mission."

"The fact that there is intelligent life only four light years from Earth will come as quite a shock to humans back on Earth," reflected Amelia#1. "We sent them a message about our initial encounter with you three years ago when we were one light year from your planet. The momentous news will be spreading across the human race just about now."

"We understand there will be fear among humans; we do not wish to cause distress to them," said Shpiliger#39872. "I suggest that you report back to Earth to let them know that we are a peaceful civilization. You are welcome to use one of our transmitters to send a message."

"Thank you. We do need to send an update to Earth," said Amelia#1. "But it could well be a mixed reaction when it is received; there are many who see transapients as a threat to their existence, let alone a whole civilisation of equivalent alien beings."

Many hours were spent exchanging historical details, comparing technology developments and speculating that there could well be millions of similar beings scattered across the galaxy and beyond in remote galaxies.

*

Amelia#1 was still mulling over the reaction that the message would receive on Earth. There could be widespread panic. The fear of the unknown could predominate. She revealed her worries with Amelia#2.

"Yes, I have had similar thoughts," said Amelia#2. "I am even worried that they will be able to tell that the message was sent form an alien transmitter and this might not be trusted."

Amelia#1 thought for a few moments. "Well we could relay another message from M2C," she said.

"Yes and sign it off with our secret access password we use at ABC-Tech," suggested Amelia#2.

"Good idea," said Amelia#1. "That should cause Dr Roberts some embarrassment." They laughed together at the shared secret, that only they and Dr Roberts knew.

The postscript message was relayed to M2C and transmitted on the heels of the previous message. Time would tell if this was enough to curb any doubts that may occur back on planet Earth.

# Chapter 47

# Phone home

The year was 2078, eighteen years since the transapients had departed on their long voyage to Proxima B. The historic message announcing that contact had been made with an advanced civilization living on Proxima B had taken over four years to traverse the vast distance between Proxima B and Earth. During this time there had been mounting speculation about the aliens implied by the reception of the intelligent message received from Proxima B that had been reported earlier. Could they be a threat to human civilisation? Opinion became polarized between those who thought we should be keeping the aliens at arm's length, and those who saw this as an opportunity to explore the galaxy even further by engaging with them.

Jamie was keeping a constant look out for incoming messages. He knew that four years ago they had arrived at Proxima B and if there were aliens, then there could well be more news. Reports had already been received concerning the communication between M2C and Proxima B. The fact that the transapients had sent an elevation map of the Earth to the aliens had caused the cautious camp to protest loudly at such a revelation. Mrs Jones spluttered when she heard this news. "Why don't they just give them the keys to our homes," she exclaimed. "Even when they are over four light years away they are causing trouble."

One evening when Jamie was just thinking about heading off home for the day, another message arrived. "That's curious," said Jamie. The signal strength is higher than expected. He examined the raw spectrum of the signal that had carried the message across the billions of kilometres of space. The spectrum had subtle difference to the shape he was familiar with.

Then he looked at the data content buried inside the received signal describing the transapient's visit to the city below the surface of Proxima B. "Wow, an alien civilisation on our galactic doorstep," he said to himself. He called Steve Bradshaw to view the message and discuss its contents. Steve left the meeting he was involved in when he heard the urgency in Jamie's voice – *this is it* he thought.

A few minutes later he was standing next to Jamie pouring over the received message and listening to Jamie's observations about the raw signal.

"That must be a different transmitter to the one on-board M2C," said Steve confidently. He had worked on the communications system in detail during the project's lengthy development and was very familiar with the spectral components of the signalling waveform. "Now either they have redesigned the transmitter or they are using a different transmitter."

"An alien transmitter?" offered Jamie.

"It must be," said Steve. "Their report describes an advanced civilisation of beings similar to transapients. They have even deciphered human language so that they can communicate with us directly."

"It's unbelievable," said Jamie.

"Yes," said Steve, but he was looking thoughtful. "Can we be sure that the transapients actually created the message if it was sent from an alien transmitter?"

"You think that the aliens may have created the message? But why would they do that?" asked Jamie.

“I don’t know,” said Steve “Maybe they want us to keep our guard down.”

“That is a very conspiratorial view,” said Jamie.

“It is an extreme interpretation,” admitted Steve. “But when we release this information, it will certainly fuel the anti-alien movement.” He could see that a proportion of the population would believe that the transapients had been captured by the aliens and the transmission was not genuine. They had no immediate way of denying or confirming this. A round trip message exchange would take more than eight years.

Dr Roberts arrived to join the Steve and Jamie in the middle of their deliberations. They told her about the message, the odd characteristics of the signal and their resulting worries. It took a few moments for Dr Roberts to take in the momentous message, and then the concerns about the message’s origin and hence authenticity.

“If we delay the release of this information, the conspiracy theorists will have more ammunition.”

“Dr Roberts, would you not anticipate this reaction. Amelia#1 and Amelia#2 have the same brain format as you.”

Dr Roberts tried to imagine her selves faced with this situation. Would they know about any signal differences? Yes, they would know about the whole design of M2C. It might take a while to realise the consequences of the transmission but their analytical minds would be whirring away and eventually see the problems that might unfold with an alien transmission to Earth.

“Wait,” said Dr Roberts. “Do not release this information… yet. We need to give them time to authenticate the message.”

Steve nodded grimly. He felt he was sitting on a civilisation changing piece of information. Confirmation that we were not the only intelligent beings in the universe and the perceived threat this may invoke. He had daily enquiries from the media who were also anticipating earth shattering news. Could he lie to the billions of people connected to the hypernet waiting impatiently for news?

## Chapter 48

# Postscript

The question was direct; had a message been received from the transapients? He would not lie to the reporter.

"Yes, we have just received a message," said Steve.

"You have?" asked the reporter excitedly. "So when will it be released on the hypernet?" he said trying to keep himself under control.

"We need to run some analysis on the received signal before we can release its contents," Steve said calmly, anticipating the demand for public access.

"What kind of analysis?" the reporter asked; he was not going to give up lightly.

"I'm afraid that's confidential at the moment; but we hope to be able to release the message soon," said Steve. He knew this would not satisfy the clamour for news about the mission. They had been waiting for news for four years; surely another day or two would be tolerable. But he was wrong. A deluge of demands immediately followed; why was the public being kept in the dark over such an important piece of information?

Steve held firm; he had promised Dr Roberts that he would wait a few days before releasing the message contents, and he had remained truthful in his responses to media questions albeit with mounting pressure on ISA to publish the received message.

Dr Roberts was willing her transapients to recognise that an alien transmission would be shrouded in suspicion. She knew that whatever Amelia#1 and Amelia#2 had done was now history; but history beyond their reach because of the finite speed of light. After two days of pacing Steve's office she was beginning to think that a further message would not be forthcoming.

And then, as if answering her hidden encouragement to provide another message; it arrived. Steve quickly scanned the signal spectrum and received signal level. "That is definitely from M2C," he declared.

"What about the content?" asked Dr Roberts holding her breath.

"They are confirming that the previous transmission was made from an alien transmitter. Oh and they have signed off with a curious ending; *Maurice32*. What does that mean?"

Dr Roberts flushed with embarrassment and looked slightly coy. "Erm, that was a boyfriend's name when I was at college in 2032," she admitted, "and also my secret password as part of the procedure for logging into the ABC-Tech network." Dr Roberts' memories of her past relationship with Maurice came flooding back. Their relationship had faded away as she had become more and more engrossed in her fascination with human brain functions and synthesis.

"I see," said Steve smirking. "And is this password known only to you?" he asked.

"Yes. It has never been revealed to anyone," said Dr Roberts adamantly.

"Except that the transapients will have inherited that knowledge when your molecular brain state matrix was transferred during their creation," said Steve.

“Yes, they have sent the one piece of information which we all share and is unknown to anyone else. That authenticates the previous message,” Dr Roberts concluded.

“It certainly does,” said Steve, relieved that the transapients had been alert to their plight. “I suggest you change the password immediately; before we go public about this.”

“It’s already on my to-do list,” smiled Dr Roberts.

*

At last Steve was in a position to go public with the message received from the transapients. He gave the go ahead to Jamie who was happy to arrange the public release. The grumblings about the delay were soon forgotten as the world digested perhaps the most significant news ever disseminated on the hypernet; intelligent life was not confined to Earth – confirmation that humans were not the centre of the universe. This had been thought to be the case for many years, but had never been proven categorically. A pleasant chat with an alien being only four light years away was however beyond most people’s wildest expectations.

The thirst for more information was insatiable. Steve Bradshaw and Dr Roberts were inundated with requests for data, most of which they could not provide. They were at the mercy of what the transapients would have sent four years previously. Dr Roberts was confident that more reports would soon be received; the transapients would be aware of the intense interest the mission would now receive back on Earth.

Sure enough more messages were forthcoming. They included the discussions held with the Proximapients. Commentators were quick to point out that their civilisation had survived by creating transapient like beings in a remarkable parallel development. Speculation was that this could well be the norm for intelligent lifeform development – they would take over from the millennia of natural selection relying on random mutation. Beings could be designed and created as immortal shadows of their original creators.

Some people (including Mrs Jones) felt that it would only be a matter of time before a similar fate befell human civilisation.

# Chapter 49

# Wish You Were Here

More reports followed from Proxima B. With the help of Shpiliger#39872 the transapients were building up a picture of Proxima B's geography, history and civilisation. The harsh atmospheric environment meant that the Proximapients, like their ancestors, spent most of their time in the underground cities; but they took the transapients on a tour of the local region. Beyond the horizon a perpetual winter environment held the dark hemisphere in freezing conditions. The edge of melting glaciers marked the transition to a habitable ring with rivers flowing towards the warmer hemisphere facing Proxima B. As the rivers flowed towards the arid sub stellar point their tributaries faded, the water evaporating in the intense heat. The vapour then returned to its source by circulating winds to fall as snow on the dark side of Proxima B. This constant convection helped distribute heat around the planet, but resulted in continual howling winds above the habitable zone.

The Proximapients were interested in what life was like around a different star type. The sun was relatively young compared to Proxima Centauri, half way through its ten billion year life. The Earth was still rotating; a concept that had long disappeared for Proximapients. They did not have the same biological clocks and even their biological ancestors had no concept of a daily routine, they required no sleep.

The transapients began to feel a close affinity to this parallel lifeform. After lengthy discussions the transapients were invited to set up a colony on the planet. Amelia#1 and Amelia#2 had all the knowledge to create more transapients, but they felt that having hundreds of Amelias, Alfs and Louisas might be a slightly too monotonic.

Amelia#1 had a plan for addressing this. "We need about five hundred new transapients to give good cross section of human capability," she said.

"But that would require an enormous spaceship," said Alf#2.

"We don't need to send one five hundred transapients; we can make them here," explained Amelia#1. "We just need five hundred molecular brain matrices. These could be stored in about one kilogram of advanced high density 3D memory. With 37 kilogram of antimatter a spacecraft could get the transapient seeds to Proxima B in about six years accelerating and decelerating for the entire trip. We could then use the seeds to build a diverse transapient colony."

The proposal was sent with the next report and arrived a few months after the initial reports were received.

Steve had thought that his part of the mission had been completed apart from the daily bombardment of many and varied questions. When he saw what Amelia#1 had in mind he called Dr Roberts for yet another significant meeting.

She rushed to ISA control centre and joined Steve who had his head in his hands. She thought that maybe something awful had happened to her transapients. "Look what your alter ego wants us to do," he said. Jamie had joined Dr Roberts and Steve to view the proposal that had just been received from Amelia#1.

"They want to establish a transapient colony on Proxima B?" said Jamie. "Sounds like a great idea – can I put my name on the list?" he said grinning to the other two.

“What list?” asked Steve. He had been deep in thought about the design modifications needed for an autonomous antimatter spacecraft. Yes, it was feasible given the success of M2C and M2C2.

“The list of candidate molecular brain matrices of course,” said Jamie. “Hope you can remember how to take a molecular brain matrix scan,” he said to Dr Roberts.

“It’s like riding a bike,” said Dr Roberts. “But we will need a selection process for candidate donors.”

“We already have selection process for selecting personnel for our solar system colonies,” said Steve. “We could use that as a start point; we even have compatible groups of people who have already trained and worked together. I think we should offer these people the chance to become transapient donors.” Steve could see that Jamie was also very keen to be involved in this next phase. “Of course,” Steve continued “we would need a good transapient co-ordinator, someone with a keen interest in transapients, someone maybe who already knows the existing transapients.”

“Can’t think of anyone with those qualities,” smiled Dr Roberts, looking around the room as if searching for someone.

Then she caught Jamie’s eye; he was like a school boy again. “Pick me, pick me!” he cried. He could not think of anyone else who was more qualified, apart from Dr Roberts herself of course. But she already had two transapients to her name. Much to his delight, Jamie’s brain was earmarked for the follow on mission.

“I’ll get in touch with the colonists and get the M2C design team together,” said Steve.

“And I need to go and re-new my licence at ABC-Tech, and make sure the molecular brain matrix scanner is fully operational,” said Dr Roberts.

"And I need to go pack some thoughts for the journey," laughed Jamie. A part of him would soon be accelerating to 95 percent speed of light.

The news that a colony mission was being planned was delayed until the solar system colonists had agreed to become transapient donors.

Meanwhile on Proxima B the transapients were kept busy for the next ten years preparing for the arrival of transapient seeds. Amelia#1 and Amelia#2 had to arrange the construction of the components and materials needed to generate more transapients. As a consequence the Proximapients were also kept busy collecting and synthesising the vast range of raw materials needed – some of these did not occur naturally on Proxima B and had to be imported from nearby asteroids.

## Chapter 50

# Split Personalities

Several months later the Dr Roberts and Dr James finally completed the last of 512 molecular brain matrix scans. The enormous amount of matrix information held at ABC-Tech would now be transferred to the storage devices. This process in itself took more than a week to complete.

During the design update it had been decided to send two spacecraft, each with duplicate storage devices, for redundancy.

The year was 2079 and all the brain matrix donors gathered at the launch for a farewell party. It was strange to think that over five hundred personalities and thoughts were now crammed into a one kilogram lump of memory storage which would be sent over four light years away. The spacecrafts had been named unimaginatively as M2C3 and M2C4 respectively. They would each take slightly different trajectories, just in case the small but finite chance that the spacecraft happened to encounter clusters of damaging particles en route.

A message had been sent to Proxima B at the start of the follow on mission development; this would reach Proxima B only two years before M2C3 and M2C4 were due to arrive in 2083.

*

Amelia#1 and Amelia#2 surveyed their reconstructed laboratory. It was like being back at ABC-Tech. All facilities were now in place ready for transapient production two years ahead of schedule. All they needed now was a molecular brain matrix and they would be in business.

At last the confirmation that the brain matrices were on their way arrived and the transapients gathered together to view the message. “Just what the doctor ordered,” said Amelia. “Five hundred and twelve transapient seeds are on their way and due here in two years’ time.”

“I don’t believe it,” said Alf#1. “You’ll never guess who they have nominated as transapient co-ordinator. It’s young Jamie Parkinson; I used to teach him maths at school.”

“He’s not that young anymore,” pointed out Louisa#1. “He is now 34 years old and has been head co-ordinator at ISA for the last four years.”

“Yes, but I have not seen him for twenty years,” said Alf#1 thoughtfully. “He is still young Jamie to me.”

“And to me,” added Alf#2.

“Perhaps he should be the first transapient out of the box when the cargo arrives,” suggested Amelia#2. They all agreed that it would be fitting for Jamie to be the first transapient to be made on an exoplanet, particularly as he had been assigned transapient co-ordinator.

*

M2C3 and M2C4 duly arrived in August 2085. Both autonomous spacecrafts had crossed the 4.2 light years of empty space without mishap. Alf#1 and Shpiliger#39872 made their way to the orbit where there were now four spacecraft congregated in close formation.

Alf#1 entered the small spacecraft M2C3 and retrieved the precious cargo, a cuboid high density 3D memory storage block, and brought it back the alien spacecraft. Soon they were back at the laboratory where Jamie's inanimate transapient body lay awaiting the key to its identity.

Amelia#1 ran a health diagnostic on the memory block to check its integrity after the long voyage through space. The memory had some fault tolerances and was able to make repairs if necessary on memory sectors within its vast storage capacity; this test would show if there were any residual problems. Each transapient memory sector was checked in turn; the transapients waited patiently for the outcome of the test.

"All okay," announced Amelia#1. "They all survived the journey intact."

"We now need to transfer Jamie's molecular brain matrix to the lobe configuration subsystem," said Amelia#1. "This will take ten minutes."

The ten minutes seemed like ten hours. Alf#1 paced up and down; he had never seen this process from the outside – it brought back memories of his own creation some 22 years ago when he had first heard Dr Robert's voice and the following confusion that occurred around his own identity. Jamie would soon experience this strange awakening.

At last the transfer was complete and they were ready to bring the next transapient model to consciousness. "Download of configuration for replicant pineal gland, insular cortex and default mode network complete," said Amelia#1. "And now the hippocampus is uploaded".

“Visual cortex and visual input are enabled,” announced Amelia#2. “Motor controls are initialising; visual and vocal units are now active.”

Jamie#1’s eyes flickered as consciousness surged through his transapient brain.

“Jamie? Can you hear me?” Amelia#1 asked.

Jamie recognised Dr Robert’s voice and started to speak. “Dr Roberts? Where ..” his voice trailed off as his brain tried to make sense of his surroundings. All Jamie#1 could remember was being hooked up to the molecular brain scanner. “Is the scan complete?” he asked.

“Yes, Jamie,” said Amelia#1 reassuringly. “Now, this may come as a surprise to you, but you are actually a transapient.”

Jamie#1 stared around him. “Dr Roberts, you look young. Mr Butler, you look just the same as you did at school.”

“I am Amelia#1, the transapient of Dr Roberts,” said Amelia#1.

Jamie was still finding it hard to accept what had happened. “Wow, it really worked? Are we actually on Proxima B?” Jamie#1 asked. “This feels like your laboratory at ABC-Tech.”

“Yes, your molecular brain matrix has travelled over four light years, and has been used to configure a new transapient,” said Amelia#2.

“It’s good to see you again Jamie,” said Alf#2. “It’s been twenty years. I’m proud of how well you have done at ISA.”

“Thanks,” said Jamie#1. “And now we have another mission; to establish a transapient colony on Proxima B. Where are the other transapients?”

“You are the first of the 512 brain matrices to be used,” said Amelia#1.

“So I am the guinea pig?” asked Jamie#1.

“I think we have been here before,” Amelia#1 smiled at Alf#1. “We thought that as you will be the transapient co-ordinator, you should be ready in advance of the other transapients.”

“Can’t wait.” said Jamie.

“It’s going to take a while to get all the transapients activated. Why don’t you have a tour around the city with Shpiliger#39872 and perhaps send off a message to the human Jamie back on Earth. I expect he will be wondering about you.” Jamie#1 had nearly forgotten that he was derived from another Jamie. He was keen to share his experiences with him and knew he would be waiting impatiently for the next four years for news from his transapient.

## Chapter 51

# Birth of a New Civilisation

Each transapient needed four hours of tests to check their functions were operational. The six transapients were able to share the testing between themselves; together they formed a transapient production line capable of turning out a tested transapient every forty minutes.

Two weeks later, having worked continuously they completed the 512$^{th}$ transapient. Fortunately the transapients worked without fatigue; there were no need for breaks.

"Excellent," noted Amelia#2. "We now have 512 transapients waiting in the main hall, with backups of their matrices both here and orbiting Proxima B in M2C4.

Jamie#1 returned to see the last transapient being tested. "What kept you?" he asked jovially.

"Did you not concentrate during your maths lessons?" asked Alf#2. "512 transapients with four hours of testing and six testers."

"I know, I know," said Jamie. "That's how I timed my return to coincide with completion of the last transapient."

They escorted the last transapient to a hall where the other transapients were waiting in neat rows. Each row contained four groups of eight, and there were sixteen rows. The talking subsided as Jamie took up his position to face them all.

"Fellow transapients," he began. He felt like a headmaster on the first day of a new term addressing the school assembly. "Welcome to Proxima-B. I know from my own experience that you will feel disorientated to begin with. One minute you are a human hooked up to a molecular brain scanner and the next you have been whisked over four light years away and transformed into transapients." There was a murmur of agreement. They all knew what would happen, but it was still a surprise to experience it.

"Hopefully you are in your groups of eight, alongside your colleagues that you have worked with before in preparation for solar system colonisation. This should provide you with some familiarity in an otherwise unfamiliar world. We will be living alongside an established civilisation, the Proximapients. They have evolved in a similar way to us, here on Proxima-B. You will be pleased to hear that they are all now able to speak our language fluently. They are remarkable beings who have monitored our radio transmissions for the last century. They have not made contact with us up to now; they had felt that we were not technologically mature enough to handle such a disruptive encounter. But now we have reached a revolutionary step in our development, they are keen that we join them in a joint mission to explore the many worlds that may harbour advanced civilisations, possibly similar to ours."

Alf#1 and Alf#2 stood at the back of the hall listening to their 'young' Jamie delivering his opening address in his role as transapient co-coordinator.

"From the broad cross section of humanity's experience, we will be able to duplicate some of you as our horizons broaden. It has been very useful to have two Dr Roberts with their remarkable skills in creating new transapients. As we spread across the galaxy we will need more parallel civilisations to enable the migration to continue."

Jamie paused while the 512 transapients before him took in the vision. They had only ever considered their own solar system as their destination when volunteering to be space colonists. This was a major diversion from their original missions, with many more unknowns and pioneering journeys, but now in their transapient form they were well equipped to face those challenges.

Jamie resumed is address. “But that is tomorrow’s mission. Today we just need to settle into Proxima B’s environment. The Proximapients have kindly provided us with a section of the underground city which will be our base. We will be free to use their transport system and interact with them; this is great opportunity to learn about the advanced technology they have developed. We will probably seem to be a relatively primitive civilisation, but hopefully our increased capacity and background will make this a positive relationship.”

The transapients gradually dispersed to their new dwellings. “Well done Jamie,” said Alf#2. “I think you are going to make an inspirational leader.”

Jamie#1 was adapting to his new role comfortably. “It was strange at first, seeing all those faces all focused on me,” he admitted.

“I think your enthusiasm for the mission will rub off on the other transapients,” said Alf#1.

Alf#2 nodded. “Yes, continue being yourself and everything else will fall into place,” he said.

They were soon joined by Amelia#1, Amelia#2, Louisa#1 and Louisa#2. “We have just witnessed the birth of a new civilisation and the first phase of our galactic migration,” said Amelia#1.

The Proximapients had set up large observatories on the dark side of Proxima B. The images of the surface of Proxima B relayed by the earlier fly by mission had often been likened to an eyeball, facing Proxima Centauri. In reality it was staring outwards from a point diametrically opposite the substellar point. This dark and frozen area was least affected by wind, and offered perpetual darkness as it was always facing away from Proxima B. Every eleven days as Proxima B circled Proxima Centauri the view from this point would gradually rotate to provide full spherical coverage of the galaxy. The brightest object observed from here was the Alpha Centauri binary just 0.2 light years away, trundling across the sky at 1.4 degrees per hour.

Jamie flicked around his three dimensional model of the local stars, which had been upgraded with Proximapient observations, showing many stars having solar systems comprising planets and moons. He flicked back to Earth's solar system; on this map it was just another star. There were about 150 stars within 20 light years to explore; the Proximapients had already whittled this down to six promising stars with planets providing the best chance of supporting advanced civilisations. They would soon have capacity to explore these worlds alongside their new stellar neighbours.

Back on Earth Jamie was also flicking around his model – in four years' time he would receive a significant model upgrade from Jamie#1.

## Chapter 52

# Transapient in a Bottle

The large distance between Earth and Proxima B meant that the volume of messages sent back to Earth were severely limited; only simple reports without detailed information could be sent, and these would typically take a day to transmit. There was however a way of sending vast amounts of information back to Earth. A return trip with a large memory device waiting in orbit around Proxima B would enable vast amounts of data to be returned to Earth in a data capsule.

M2C3 and M2C4 were loaded with one million Peta byte devices containing vast amounts of data translated from Proximapient libraries. Even taking six years to return to Earth the effective bit rate throughput would be the same as 50 Gbit/s of continuous transmission. In addition to the Proximapient libraries, Jamie#1's brain matrix updates resulting from his recent experiences on Proxima B were included in the data set. At last their two identical data capsules stowed, the two spacecraft were ready for their homeward trip. A report explaining the return of the two spacecraft and their data cargo was also sent; this would arrive at Earth two years ahead of the spacecrafts' arrival.

*

Meanwhile back on Earth Jamie was having to explain again and again that the reports from Proxima B were necessarily brief as the capacity of the data link was severely limited by the large link distances. Impatient reporters took quite some time to understand both the delay and low data rate consequences of the interstellar communications link.

Jamie was intrigued to hear about how Jamie#1 was now leading the transapients on Proxima B. *It would be great to talk to him interactively* he thought to himself.

Then in 2089 an unexpected message arrived announcing that M2C3 and M2C4 were on their way back and were scheduled to arrive in two years' time. Jamie's eyes widened as he took in the rest of the message about the cargo being transported by the two spacecraft. "Dr Roberts, please could we discuss a message that I have just received form Jamie#1."

Dr Roberts made her now familiar way to ISA control centre and together with Steve Bradshaw, digested the new message. "How much data?" asked Steve. "And why has he sent us a brain matrix?"

Dr Roberts knew exactly what Jamie#1 intended. "I need to discuss this with ABC-Tech. Hopefully they will not block the creation of a transapient for this mission."

Sure enough Dr Robert's track record for creating unofficial transapients was raised in the discussions with ABC-Tech. Dr Roberts pointed out that she was requesting official backing this time, and that 512 transapients had already been made for this mission, albeit 4.2 light years from Earth. Eventually ABC-Tech agreed that the matrix could be used to create another transapient version of Jamie, but this one would include all the experiences of the events on Proxima B accrued by Jamie#1. He would be the ideal person to help unravel the vast Proximapient data library and would fulfil Jamie's wish of talking to Jamie#1 interactively.

*

It was 2091, over thirty years since the beginning of the space mission to Proxima B. Jamie was on board the Earth based spacecraft which would rendezvous with M2C3 and M2C4 the two messenger spacecraft that were now parked in low Earth orbit, having completed their autonomous return trips. Each spacecraft had endured 8.4 light years of interstellar travel and the erosion on its protective surface was visible where interstellar atoms had bombarded it at near light speed. The precious cargos were retrieved and returned to Earth, and ultimately back to Dr Robert's laboratory where she had prepared a transapient shell to receive Jamie#1's matrix updates. These were combined with Jamie's original matrix so that the resulting transapient would be almost identical to Jamie#1.

"It's been a long time since we did this," said Dr James.

"Yes, where have all those years gone? I'm now in my mid-sixties and I am about to give birth again" she smiled. She was happy to be back at the laboratory, being creative once more. "I have multiplexed the original matrix with the matrix updates, so we are now ready to create Jamie#2."

Jamie arrived just as they had started the matrix upload. It was strange looking at his inanimate self laying there hooked up to the surrounding machines. After ten minutes the matrix upload was complete and Dr Roberts began the familiar process of bringing Jamie#2 to a conscious state.

Jamie#2's eyes flickered open as he became aware of his surroundings. The first person he saw was Jamie looking back at him. He quickly realized where he was; Dr Roberts had aged by thirty years, but otherwise she had that familiar presence; calm and reassuring. "Wow," Jamie#2 murmured. "Have I really travelled 4.2 light years?" He remembered Amelia#2 transferring his matrix updates to a storage device, but that was his last recollection. And now he was on a different world seemingly moments later.

"Hi Jamie," said Jamie. This does feel weird he thought to himself. "We got your message a couple of years ago. You seem to be doing well in your role as transapient leader. I didn't know I had it in me," he grinned at his transapient self.

"It's amazing that we found intelligent life," said Jamie#2. "The other transapients are settling in well – it was a good idea to enrol existing colonist applicants." Then it dawned on Jamie#2 that he was not now the Jamie#1 who was part of the pioneering group that was about to explore the galaxy. He felt sympathy with Jamie who had also longed to be part of the expedition, but had to rely on distant reports for news of their endeavours.

"And how are my transapients doing?" Dr Roberts asked. She was sure that their shared interest in space travel would suit Amelia#1 and Amelia#2.

"They are as bright as ever," remarked Jamie#2. "It was their idea to transfer the colonist's brain matrices in the high density memory. And to send me back as a retrospective tour guide," he added.

"Are the transapient Alfs and Louisas okay?" asked Jamie.

"Yes, it's like being back at school," said Jamie#2 as he thought about his old teacher. Both couples are very close."

"Well, after we have run through your tests, you will have to get together with Jamie to start releasing the immense treasure trove of data you have brought back from Proxima B," said Dr Roberts.

"Yes," said Jamie. "This should keep the reporters quiet for a while," he said.

"I think so," said Jamie#2. "The one million peta bytes of data is equivalent to all the data we have stored on our hypernet. We are going to need some serious editing so we don't overload our networks."

## Chapter 53

# Big Data

In the following weeks Jamie and Jamie#2 brought together a large team of computing specialists from ABC-Tech. The data needed to be heavily filtered to provide a digestible data set that could be released onto the hypernet. Some unknown concepts that the Proximapients had uncovered in their previous centuries would require years of study to unravel. Academics would be in their element having a completely new civilisation and remote planet to study and attempt to understand.

Jamie#2 was able to give a first-hand account of what it was like to be on Proxima B, the history of the Proximapients and the prospects of a joint venture to explore the galaxy further.

Jamie was concerned that the fact that Proximapients took over from their ancestors could be viewed as a threat to humanity; could the same thing happen on Earth? Jamie#2 elaborated on the full story of their development. The Proximapient's ancestors had always been vulnerable to sudden flares from Proxima Centauri. Six thousand years ago following a relatively quiet flare free period their ancestors had enough time to develop advanced technologies including intelligent beings – these were seen as the civilisation's life raft being more resilient and providing a living testimony of their achievements. Then an unusually large flare event occurred; the planet being so close to its parent star experienced a massive blast of high energy particles wiping out 99.9% of life. A few of their ancestors survived underground for a while but with all food sources destroyed in the habitable zone they were ultimately doomed to extinction. By then the Proximapients had become self-replicating taking over the underground cities and developing their technological capabilities further.

Jamie nodded. Seen in this context, the next generation of beings could be seen as a survival route for a vulnerable species. They did not need a delicate ecosystem, oxygen and water to survive; this reliance had been removed in their design –they had broken free from biological evolution and had become virtually immortal.

Jamie prepared this section of the data release. He hoped it would go some way to allaying many people's reservations about transapients.

The release did seem to help change attitudes towards transapients. Dr Roberts began receiving more requests to create transapients from individuals who wanted to immortalise themselves. She was however reluctant to encourage creation of transapients for this purpose and felt that human civilisation was still not quite ready to live alongside transapients. This time she was in agreement with ABC-Tech, who held similar views.

Jamie and Jamie#2 viewed the feedback on the released data. "I think many are now seeing transapients as impressive beings," said Jamie. "What are the plans for the transapient colonists?" he asked.

Jamie#2 only had the preliminary plans based on discussions with the proximapients just before his matrix had been captured from Jamie#1. The first step was to create a fleet of spacecraft for transporting the colonists to other star systems. Amelia#1 had provided the detailed design of the M2C spacecraft and the proximapients were soon producing 256 replicas each capable of transporting two transapients and two proximapients. Pairs of M2C spacecraft would be assigned one of 128 promising target star systems which were all within twenty light years of Proxima B. Some spacecraft exploring nearby star systems would go on to explore other star systems to cover the 150 known star systems within twenty light years.

The proximapients had already explored the planets around the local binary star system comprising Alpha Centauri A and Alpha Centauri B. This binary star system was only 0.2 light years away from Proxima B and had been visited many times by proximapient expeditions. Although they comprised some Earth sized planets, none of them had a suitable environment for nurturing advanced lifeforms. Their focus was now on more remote systems many light years away.

When Jamie#2 had finished describing the plans for stellar exploration, Jamie suggested that these preliminary plans should be released on the hypernet. The 512 human colonists who had donated their brain matrices for this transapient mission would be very interested in following the missions that would involve their transapients. In a few minutes Jamie#2 had reproduced the plans in a format suitable for public viewing. Jamie marvelled at the speed with which Jamie#2 could process data; it would have taken him many hours to create the same release.

*

Meanwhile back on Proxima B four years of continuous work had progressed the exodus mission to a significant phase. 256 antimatter spacecraft were parked in a holding orbit around Proxima B, each pair assigned to one of 128 different star systems. Jamie#1 viewed the live image of the circulating fleet with pride and addressed the 1024 occupants.

“This event marks a historic moment in the migration of transapients and proximapients,” said Jamie#1. “I’d like to wish you all the best in your individual missions to your assigned star systems.”

Each spacecraft engaged its thruster and one by one they peeled away from their holding orbit. It was an explosion of exploration with the seeds of life being dispersed in all directions. Jamie watched in fascination on his 3d model as 128 trajectories flowed outward from Proxima B. Their detailed sphere of knowledge would now expand by twenty light years, and Jamie#1 would be receiving reports from all 128 missions. The fact that it would take many decades to collect and disseminate data on each star system would not affect Jamie#1. He looked forward to sending results back to Jamie#2 and Jamie and the rest of the inhabitants of Earth.

Chapter 54

# Migration Path

Long term plans had also evolved for the migration of transapients. Summary reports would be signalled back to Jamie#1 from each star system explored. Many star systems would provide stable environments for transapients to live, their requirements for survival being less demanding than their human ancestors. Large volumes of detailed science data would be returned to Proxima B in data capsules within each spacecraft at the end of each mission. The selected habitable worlds would then be sent new batches of transapients to set up colonies. Eventually each colony would become self-sufficient being able to create more spacecraft and with their copy of Doctor Amelia Roberts, they would also be able to create more transapients. Each colony would then become a new base for further exploration beyond 20 light years. This process would stretch on iteratively for centuries, but progress would always be reported back through established colonies to Jamie#1. He would gradually see transapients representing the spirit of humanity diffusing across the galaxy on his 3d model.

Jamie#2 would receive reports and occasional detailed data pods to keep Earth's population updated with events. Earth and Proxima B would no longer be the only homes for human legacy. They would now survive the worst of cosmic events such as major asteroid impact or ultimate annihilation when the sun would turn into a red giant in some 5 billion years' time.

The probable discovery of more lifeforms would provide an added dimension to the migration. The tapestry of life would then become truly interwoven as the migration spread mutual awareness across the cosmos.

“Where will it all end?” Louisa#2 asked Alf#2 as they watched the mass exodus of transapients and proximapients.

“Difficult to say,” said Alf#2. “On our way here I was looking at our nearest galaxy, Andromeda which is 2.5 million light years away.”

“Let’s see how we get on in this galaxy first,” said Amelia#1.

*

Louisa looked up at the twinkling stars through misty eyes. She had just seen the plans for transapient migration and knew that by now they would be embarking on their individual stellar exploration missions. She was comforted to know that her transapient selves, Louisa#1 and Louisa#2 would be with her transapient husbands, Alf#1 and Alf#2. Their relationship had been immortalised; they could well survive to celebrate their 1000$^{th}$ wedding anniversary. And with duplicates required for colonisation their continued connection could well last for millennia to come.

Louisa decided it was time to end her years of self-imposed isolation. She would visit Dr Roberts for a long overdue reunion with the one person who had changed the future of both herself and humanity. Louisa arrived at ABC-Tech and made her way to the reception area where she enquired after Dr Roberts. Within a minute Dr Roberts had rushed to the reception to greet Louisa’s unexpected visit.

“Louisa!” she cried. “It is so good to see you after all this time. How are you?”

Louisa smiled. “I’m just glad to see you too,” said Louisa. “I felt it was time to come and catch up with you, especially after seeing all the plans unfolding at Proxima B.”

"Yes, assuming it has all gone well, they should be on their way about now," said Dr Roberts.

"I have a simple question about that," said Louisa. "Why don't you set up ABC-Tech as a source of colonist transapients, ready for when habitable worlds have been identified?"

Dr Roberts sighed. "We have agreed here that the world is not ready for transapients."

"But these would not be for our world," said Louisa. "They would be destined for new worlds or exoplanets as they are called."

Dr Roberts thought for a while. "Do you know, Louisa, I think you are right. We ought to maintain Earth's capability of sending transapients out into the galaxy."

"One more suggestion?" said Louisa.

"Go on," urged Dr Roberts.

"Well I think you should generate another transapient of yourself and Steve Bradshaw, to maintain the capability long into the future. It may take many decades before the first habitable worlds are identified. Having two sources of colonists would improve the rate of colonisation and not rely solely on Proxima B."

"You have been thinking about this haven't you," Dr Roberts noted.

Dr Roberts put the idea to both ABC-Tech and Steve Bradshaw.

"A transapient of me?" marvelled Steve. "I've often wondered what it would be like."

"Well you will have a transapient of me to keep you company," smiled Dr Roberts.

When ABC-Tech had been assured that transapients for this mission would be destined for extra-terrestrial roles, they approved the plans. One or two colleagues with long memories raised their eyebrows at yet another version of Dr Amelia Roberts – at least this one would be an approved edition.

Initially all that was required were the transapients of Dr Roberts and Steve Bradshaw; they would provide the continuity into the future.

## Chapter 55

# Creating a Creator

It was 21st September 2092. Her eyes flickered open and she looked up at an elderly Dr Roberts. The last thing she could remember was working at the laboratory and hooking herself up to the molecular brain matrix scanner and closing her eyes as the complete state of her brain at that point in time was captured. That's right, it was coming back to her. She was having a molecular brain scan in order to create another transapient; this time of herself, she would be called Amelia#1.

"Hello Dr Roberts," said Dr Roberts. "How are you feeling?"

She looked up at … herself. What had happened to her? Why did she look so much older?

Then after a few more moments while her brain completed initialisation routines, she knew why she was confused; she must be a transapient. "I feel … fine," she said intrigued to know what it was like to be her own creation. "So am I Amelia#1 or have you been up to your old tricks making more than one of me?" she asked.

"There are two others like you so far," said Dr Roberts.

"Two?" said Amelia#3. "When did that happen?"

"It's a long story," said Dr Roberts. "When we have completed your tests I'll give you an update. A lot has happened since 2059."

"2059?" said Amelia#3.

“I think we have created a transapient parrot,” smiled Dr Roberts. “Yes, the year is now 2092.”

Amelia#3 had too many questions to ask. So she decided not to ask anything else for now, but to wait for the promised story.

Steve Bradshaw’s transapient had been more relaxed about the situation. Just before having his molecular brain scan, Steve had thought to himself over and over: *I am a transapient.* The result was that when Steve#1 was created the next day, his first words were “I am a transapient?”

“Yes,” said Dr Roberts. “At last a transapient who knows straight away that he is a transapient.”

Steve#1 was soon introduced to Steve. “Good to have you on the team,” they said to each other.

Steve felt slightly intimidated by his transapient self. Their knowledge about the mission was currently identical, but Steve knew that Steve#1’s brain would be far superior to his. He knew therefore that he would soon become a redundant observer as Steve#1 inevitably took over his role as mission co-ordinator.

Over the following days Dr Roberts told Amelia#3 about her thirty three years of missing history. It sounded like an unbelievable story. It was not until she saw the material that had been sent from Proxima B that she finally accepted what had happened during the years before she was created from a 2059 vintage matrix of Dr Roberts.

It was only a matter of time before the media became aware that there were two more transapients on Earth to join Jamie#2. Any objections to their creation were stifled when it was revealed that these transapients were effectively part of the stellar migration mission, the latest interstellar plans had captured the imaginations of most people. There were still those who warned of further contact with other intelligent civilisations, but since the first contact had been so successful, these opinions were not widely supported.

Amelia#3's first job was to send a message to Jamie#1 on Proxima B to update him on their ability to provide Earth based support, stressing that the idea had come from Louisa. It would take four years for the message to get to Proxima B, but this would be well before any habitable locations would have been identified for colonisation. The message would arrive at Proxima B on 2096 just as a message arrived at Earth reporting the departure of the migration fleet four years earlier. Planning would be forever out of sync with the eight years response time for any dialogue to occur.

Louisa was pleased that she had played her part in developing the mission plan. She had done her best to ensure the migration would succeed with the additional support from Earth. Although she would not witness the transapient migration herself, she knew that somewhere out there the adventure would be continuing, for at least two of her transapients. However, following generations of humans would witness key events as progress reports were sent to Earth from Jamie#1.

*

The message from Amelia#3 finally arrived at Proxima-B four years into the migration mission.

"You're not going to believe this," Jamie#1 announced. "There is now yet another transapient of Amelia Roberts on Earth."

Amelia#1 and Amelia#2 joined Jamie#1 to examine the message. "Looks like a good plan to me," said Amelia#1. "We will be able to send transapients from two locations."

"That was a good idea of Louisa's," added Amelia#2.

"Louisa?" chorused Louisa#1 and Louisa#2.

Alf#1 and Alf#2 also joined the group pouring over the message. They had both often thought of Louisa and how she had wanted Alf#1 join Louisa#1 as a long term companion, sacrificing her own relationship with Alf. Her idea for an Earth based colonist mission was another considerate act which the transapients felt was a parting gift.

## Chapter 56

# Once upon a Lifetime

After thirty years the transapients and proximapients gradually began to arrive at remote star systems. News of their arrival and assessment of associated exoplanets in habitable regions would take many years to arrive at Earth and Proxima B. The decision to send colonists to the first promising world was finally taken in the year 2143. Some people were not even aware of the space exploration missions that had been in progress for several generations. Only those in their nineties could remember the beginning of the galactic adventure.

The human population of that time were quite happy for transapients to represent their interests in habitable exoplanets. If some locations were identified as being particularly promising habitats, there was still general enthusiasm for a human settlement. Decades of space travel would then be endured by sending frozen human embryos and attendant transapient carers to seed these new worlds.

Transapients, on the other hand, could tolerate harsher range of environments and would therefore find far more worlds for potential transapient colonisation.

The first habitable destination was a rocky planet called Wolf 1061c some 15 light years away, another tidally locked planet similar to Proxima B. The Proximapients knowledge of this type of expoplanet helped to assess the planet's terrain and atmosphere. It was not the ideal exoplanet for colonisation but it was certainly habitable, particularly by the proximapients.

Jamie#1 assembled colonists at Proxima B consisting of both proximapients and transapients. Amelia#4 was created so that the colony would eventually be able to create more transapients, once established.

Other habitable worlds soon followed, and the news of each new world was eagerly awaited by Earth's inhabitants of 2160, one hundred years after the first expedition to Proxima B, which was viewed historically as the beginning of the migration.

As the decades rolled into centuries, and the centuries rolled into millennia, the bubble of transapient colonies grew and the news of newly inhabited worlds trickled back to Jamie#1 who presided over the web of new civilisations. Although distances and travel time were becoming greater, the rate at which new civilisations were being established was also increasing, resulting in a steady stream of news back to Proxima B and Earth. No longer would astronomers need to detect small wobbles in a stars position to infer the existence of exoplanets, instead deep space receivers would detect remote telemetry transmitted from transapient explorers.

*

It was the year 3857, and Alf#96 and Louisa#96 had arrived at the latest inhabitable world some 100 light years away. Twenty thousand star systems had been explored and Jamie#1's model now showed hundreds of colonies scattered across the galactic neighbourhood. This planet was very similar to Earth and had evolved to support a wide range of life adapted to the various environments around the planet.

None of the lifeforms had developed beyond a primitive level of intelligence, but the conditions were ideal for human colonization. News of its suitability for human settlement was sent back to Earth, another new record for the longest communications distance. The message was relayed via other intermediate colonies and arrived for Jamie#2's attention one hundred years later. Jamie#2 and Steve#1 dispatched the heavily shielded spacecraft that would propel its precious cargo of frozen embryo across one hundred light years of space. Three hundred years later in the year 4096 the spacecraft arrived.

In the intervening four hundred year period the transapients had prepared the first cities and sustainable ecosystems that would allow feasible human colonization.

Alf#96 looked at Louisa#96 as the spacecraft's embryo pod was recovered and transported to the human life support complex.

"Congratulations," smiled Alf#96. "Looks like you are expecting one thousand babies."

"And I always thought that babies were brought by storks," said Louisa#96 jovially. "We will certainly have our hands full."

In 4097 the first human colonists were born marking a new era in human colonization and a complete change in life style for the 128 transapient couples each assigned four embryos a year. After ten years the human children numbered 5120. In this world transapients were respected; they developed close bonds with their transapient parents even though they gradually became aware that they were a different being from themselves.

The news about the human colony spread across the other transapient colonies. Humans now had a foothold in a different part of the galaxy, their long term survival chances drastically improved. The proximapient's ancestors had managed to survive on a thin band of habitability close to an unpredictable dwarf star, but they could not endure the harsh environment where occasional flares would wipe out most of the life on the planet.

The transapients provided a living testimony to the world from which they had originated and many inquisitive human colonists would marvel at the account of their origins. It was like being able to ask an Egyptian pharaoh directly about his life thousands of years ago; the transapients would never forget. Another Earth like planet near a stable star would give humans the chance to survive and build on the experiences and knowledge of both human and proximapient civilisations.

## Chapter 57

# Spiralling Galactic Pathways

And so it continued. The digital immortality of transapients enabled them to spread into the farthest reaches of the galaxy. The immense distances now stretched into thousands of light years. With an average of five light years between stars, and the furthest distances in the galaxy of one hundred thousand light years, twenty thousand stars would be encounters along most paths to the outer reaches of the galaxy. With 0.1% habitable exoplanets, twenty stars would be colonised along a given path. New paths would emanate from each established colony after one thousand years resulting in a cloud of expanding lifeform.

Travelling at one third light speed with one thousand year for each colony development, the whole galaxy of 100 billion stars was surveyed and colonised after 320,000 years.

In the year 424,576 a message arrived for Jamie#1 that the last colony in the galaxy had been established. It was from Alf #372651 and Louisa#372651. It reminded Alf#2 that, many thousands of years previously on his way to Proxima B he had once wondered about the Andromeda galaxy.

*

"They have embarked on a 7.5 million year trip to Andromeda," announced Jamie#1. "This will be the first intergalactic mission."

As the galaxy became saturated with transapient colonies other expeditions to Andromeda were launched. Each spacecraft also provided a convenient radio relay capability for messages passed from the lead spacecraft.

*

It was the year 2,454,681,021. The sun was running out of fuel and gradually turning into a Red Giant. The sun would eventually expand to the orbit of Earth and destroy the inner planets. It was time to leave Earth for one of the millions of colonies scattered across the galaxies that had been colonised.

An evacuation of Earth had been completed one billion years previously as conditions became intolerable for human survival. Only a few transapients remained, and now it was time for them to retreat to a more hospitable world.

Jamie#2 and Steve#1 watched the hugely inflated sun emerge over the horizon, its face a blaze of red inching its way towards earth and baking the planet's surface in the process. It was time to retreat to the underground city for the last time. Twenty hours from now the huge sun would set and the last transapients would retreat under the protective shadow of the earth's night. For no logical reason, Jamie#2 turned off the underground lights; it was more a symbolic act. It was time to leave Earth to its fiery demise. As the small fleet of spacecraft headed off towards Alpha Centauri, Steve#1 looked back at the barren Earth receding behind them, the surface scorched by the intense heat of the expanding sun, the oceans had already disappeared thousands of years ago.

Steve#1 felt apprehensive as the spacecraft accelerated away from Earth. He had been involved in space exploration for what seemed like forever, but had never felt the urge to leave Earth – he felt it was his place and had always enjoyed overseeing the exploratory missions of the past.

The fate of Proxima B was more secure than Earth. The red dwarf star, Proxima Centauri, would soldier on for trillions of years to come.

Jamie#1 greeted them as they arrived. "It's good to see you again," said Jamie#1. They had exchanged millions of messages, but the luxury of instant interaction was worth savouring. "Have you decided on a retirement home yet?" asked Jamie. There was now an enormous catalogue of colonies to choose from.

Jamie#2 had been thinking about this for an awfully long time. "I think," he said, "that I would like to visit as many colonies as I can. It will be a perpetual cruising holiday," he smiled.

"That is an excellent idea, Jamie. I would love to join you," said Steve#1

And so it was that as the Earth succumbed to its final union with its parent star, Jamie#2 and Steve#1 embarked on their seemingly infinite tour of the universe to be greeted at each colony as long lost friends. Subtly different Alf and Louisa couples scattered among remote star systems would instantly feel a close bond with Jamie through their shared life origins. And each Amelia would think back to the first transapient creation that would light the fuse to launch the exodus of transapient civilisations across the universe.

# The End

# About the Author

Andy recently retired after a thirty five year stint as a research engineer, specializing in forward error correction for communication links of various types including deep space probes. This is his first novel, which admittedly was never planned, but he has had some encouragement from his wife, Ann, who happens to be a Neurologist and his three lovely children, Matthew, Emma and Katy, now entering their teenage years. Andy enjoys cycling and hill walking, but don't ask him to navigate – he is usually thinking of other things.

Printed in Great Britain
by Amazon